Y0-BSS-797

STORIES BY

The Way to Cobbs Creek

D A B N E Y S T U A R T

UNIVERSITY OF MISSOURI PRESS
Columbia and London

Copyright © 1997 by Dabney Stuart
University of Missouri Press, Columbia, Missouri 65201
Printed and bound in the United States of America
All rights reserved
5   4   3   2   1   01   00   99   98   97

Library of Congress Cataloging-in-Publication Data
Stuart, Dabney, 1937–
     The way to Cobbs Creek : stories / Dabney Stuart.
        p.   cm.
     Contents: The way to Cobbs Creek—Bright wings—Mariah—
The air ghosts breathe.
     ISBN 0-8262-1143-7 (pbk. : alk. paper)
     I. Title.
PS3569.T8W39   1997
813'.54—dc21   97-27183
                                                                                      CIP

♾ ™ This paper meets the requirements of the
American National Standard for Permanence of Paper
for Printed Library Materials, Z39.48, 1984.

Cover Design: Susan Ferber
Text Design: Mindy Shouse
Typesetter: BOOKCOMP
Printer and binder: Thomson-Shore, Inc.
Typeface: Giovanni Book

for Sandra
and in memory of
Tuggie Stuart
and
L. M. vonSchilling

Contents

The Way to Cobbs Creek

The Way to Cobbs Creek

This is your proper countenance
and yet the lines of your father's
face may lie deep and invisible here.
— Peter Ackroyd

A man who does not exist,
A man who is but a dream.
— W. B. Yeats

The four-pound-test monofilament spun almost invisibly from her rod, carrying on its outward arc the curl it bore on the reel, having been so long wound there, unused. It settled that way on the river's surface, too, a looping, hair-raising ride if not for the tiniest homunculus then for a newly hatched fly. To whiz through the tube that coiled line traced would have thrilled any daredevil mite brave enough to chance it.

Any word willowy enough to have shivered through the air that way could become the air's auger, too, the supple heir to and embodiment of its wispiest touches.

Yvette Wu was a new friend of ours. She was a Chinese expatriate who had come from Mao's jails and reeducation camps via Hong Kong, to this western Virginia riverside in May, and was learning to fish. In ten minutes she had become familiar with the basic movements of spin casting. She had also added an angle or two of her own:

a subtle shift of her body's address to the river after she had laid the lure on its surface, a sixteenth turn at most, but enough to say "I

1

*am one way with you when this strange American assembly of hooks
and shine is flying toward you, and another way when it rests upon
your back";*

*and a little pop of her jaw the two times she caught something, audible
but fleeting, delicately sharp, accompanied by a swift dimple about the
size of a piece of barley in her left cheek.*

When she pulled the first three-inch bluegill over the rocks at the water's
edge and up onto the grass, her mouth, diminutive even in so slight a body
and face—structured of bones that sometimes seemed as thin as angel
hair—formed the smallest of O's, holding that shape until the fish was
free of the lure and lay in her palm, covering it.

She bowed over this creature she had captured—called a pumpkinseed
after its shape and spotted orange belly—hand and fish held out in surprise
and delight and curiosity. From the side she resembled a religious figure,
bent in reverence, her body itself a bow, her arm seeming paradoxically to
pierce her.

When I asked her if she wanted to release the fish back into the water
herself, or let me do it, she turned her head to me.

No other part of her moved; her body retained its posture of protection
and offering.

"Release?"

"Yes. It's too small to keep."

Her face, mobile in inverse proportion to its size, went through a series
of expressions like water across which the breeze wavers: shock, denial,
perplexity, resignation, and finally a combining of realization and what
I took to be amusement. During this chameleonic display her mouth
resumed its O; she revealed her inner concatenation through her facial
muscles and her eyes—

lustrous, black, like the bluegill's eyes, repeating in the shape of iris and
cornea the nearly perfect circle her mouth sustained; indeed, it seemed
her eyes spun their own coil inward, complements of the roundness of
her face and head and mouth, drawing me through the swift tunnel of
her reactions.

"Too small to eat, yes?"

"Yes. There's hardly anything left after you clean so little a fish."

"So little fish," she said, turning so she seemed to address the pumpkinseed. "We keep." Then, speaking to me again, "You have place to keep, Mark?"

"We can use the extra cooler."

With this her body straightened to its full height—five feet, two inches. She gave me safekeeping of her fish, tilting her hand so it slid into mine.

She scooped some river water into the cooler and set it on the ground beside us; we reversed the transfer of the fish, and she released it into its new containment, squatting beside it, curled, compact —
ceremonious, beautiful.

She landed one more, almost a replica of the first, and slipped it into the white Styrofoam rectangle whose blue speckles looked like part of the water the two little fish swam in.

When we got home she cleaned, but didn't behead, the fish, and poached them in a six-inch skillet, in white wine to cover, seasoned with ginger and a few drops of soy sauce.

They were delicious beyond my comprehension—a whole other culture given to me not only in Yvette Wu's sinuously muscular will and the elated compression of her body and its attention to the pores of the world, but in the savor of that delicate white flesh as well—exotic, though it had been taken from, so to speak, my own backyard.

There were only three of us—Yvette, my new wife Callie, and I—not five thousand, who partook of this meal, and it would be too much to say we were filled, but nonetheless I felt I had tasted a portion of that miracle.

WE STARTED fishing early, my brother Luke and I, not because it was something we decided to do, or even wanted to do, but because, simply put, there was water at the foot of our grandparents' front yard, and we were children who needed to be kept occupied. Family heritage played a part in it as well, but there, too, the daily proximity of water into which the participants—my grandfather and, later, my father, by marriage, as it were—had been accidentally placed, was determinant.

Skill and competition were inextricably tangled into Luke's and my first forays into this deliciously messy activity. Given the almost six-year gulf between us, it was inevitable that I would dominate my five- and six- and seven-year-old brother and, because that was so easy, that I would begin to compete with myself.

Our routine, designed by our grandfather, couldn't have been simpler, a tribute to the quality of his attention to us, derived, I'm convinced, from the undaunted survival of his own childlike spirit and sense of mischief. In his early sixties, he would get down on the rug and be bronco to Luke's cowboy (as he had done for me years back, during the period when he'd saved me from drowning), play hide-and-seek indoors and out in the evenings when he came home from his insurance office, make crazy comic-strip drawings featuring both of us—crossing the Delaware with George Washington, discovering the South Pole, daring the galaxy in space ships, but most often the two of us sitting on a boat or a dock or the side of a bridge, fishing.

My favorite times with my grandfather, ever since I was coordinated enough to manage a hammer and a screwdriver, occurred in his garage, an L-shaped building set well away from the big house. One leg of the L was crammed with junk: short boards of all sizes and degrees of desuetude, a row of pulleys hanging along the edge of a rafter, wires of all lengths and thicknesses enovalling nails dotted on the windowless north wall, nails and nuts and bolts in containers from baby-food jars to coffee cans, five-gallon pickle jugs filled with linseed oil and turpentine and other exotic, breathtaking unguents, two old woodsmen's crosscut saws, rusted and pocked but whose monstrous gawking teeth stretched across the row of windows facing south were still the stuff of nightmares. On the rafters above lay the long boards. And in a special section of the south wall, between the windows and the inner corner of the L where his work bench ended, his fishing rods leaned in a row. They seemed huge to me, and numberless, some so big it would take a giant to wield them.

The other leg of the L housed the cream and maroon Nash turtle-back, the vehicular design of the period, the height of sleekness and aerodynamics but looking to me like a bulbous creature that would squeeze upwards and flatten, cartoon style, if driven too fast into the wind. When my (he was *my* grandfather when we labored in the garage together, not the least important aspect of those sessions being the annihilation of little brothers) grandfather worked at his bench he backed the car out onto the garage apron, opening the whole section to the air and light.

While he tinkered with whatever project he had going I would have the run of the place. I'd usually end up, despite my mother's litany of prohibitions that preceded my release to this unwholesome place, somehow seated in the traces of oil and sludge left on the concrete floor, pounding #12 nails into blocks of awkwardly different thicknesses, rarely connecting them. Shipbuilding, my grandfather called it.

"How're you coming with that ship, Mark?" was his refrain question when he'd interrupt himself and walk over to join me. He'd squat down and examine the blocks with four or five nails sticking out of them, like antennae. "Where's the rudder?" he'd ask, or "Where's the bridge?" and thus I'd learn things, too. It was the best school I ever attended.

He never sat down with me in the grease spots, as if that were my special portion of the place. After our consultation he'd run a finger through the deep black stain, straighten up, stretch, look down at me and smile. I took it then as an expression of his pleasure in our being together, and in me, an acceptance no one else knew quite how to offer. Now I like to think it involved as well his sense of our conspiracy against the women who would keep us clean—dolls on a shelf to be trotted out to impress company—of which cohort my mother, his daughter, was commander-in-chief.

Our routines were uncomplicated until Luke got big enough to want to tag along with me wherever I went. After his post-lunch nap became a historical oddity his presence grew into an interminable annoyance. Our grandfather did his best to treat us equally; one way of doing this was to set us up as fishermen.

He used a length of light line, one end attached to a cane pole, the other tied through the eye of a small hook. The rig worked like a long-handled quirt: we would thrash the hook—baited with the insides of a snail we'd pick off the concrete breakwater at the foot of the yard, and squash with a rock—into the water, about three-feet deep at high tide, and let it sink. When a minnow tugged the line we'd repeat the motion in reverse, flinging our quarry into the grass.

Occasionally we'd land a blue crab this way, the ensuing chase a combination of fear and curiosity and the exercise of power, watching its jagged flight eventually, unerringly, end as it scratched its way across the two-foot width of the breakwater and into the bay again.

Nothing ever stayed on the hook, making the grappling with the minnow on land more exciting than the actual engagement with it in the water, though that initiating tug was a thrill. I remember loving the arc of the minnow as it left the hook, somewhere around twelve or one o'clock, turning nose over tail through the air, a black whirligig against the overcast sky, as if I were looking at a spinning alien shape inside a kaleidoscope. When it landed in the grass it was a minnow again, flopping against the firm ground in a motion totally different from its brief, endeavoring flight.

My heart seemed to go with it in both places, soaring, and struggling to get back home.

Luke would usually pull too hard, snatching the hook from the minnow's mouth—which rarely touched the hook, closing only against the burl of snail hiding it—or let the minnow run about at the end of his line as if he were giving it a ride at a carnival concession. Sometimes he didn't notice he'd caught anything until I asked him what he was dreaming about. On those occasions we'd have to get Granddad to come and remove the hook with his needle-nosed pliers.

I kept score. When we'd put the rods next to his in the garage— miniatures mimicking, or aspiring to, the real, serious thing—the tally was always heavily in my favor, a *rout*, which terse, accusing word I'd picked up from a headline on the sports pages of the *Daily Press*.

I'd keep a list, too, of our daily catch—though that's misleading since we fished only two or three days a week, being refused the game often enough to keep us interested in it. After four or five entries I began to omit Luke's number and rack up only my own impressive total on the sheet of my grandfather's business stationery he'd tacked on the garage-door frame. After breaking my own record became a routine, I began taking a ruler to the breakwater and measuring the plumper and longer of the minnows I cast into the grass, itself an achievement, given their slippery elusiveness.

The largest I had landed by somewhere in late July of my thirteenth year in the second summer of the game we called Breakwater Bites, was slightly over six inches. The usual length was four to five inches, often smaller; to approach six, let alone surpass it by a hair, was rare indeed.

But, as Luke proved one afternoon, not rare enough. By some cosmic fluke—as if all the astrological bodies and forces, both impelling and repelling ("My right hand attracts, my left hand repels," as one of my favorite comic-book heroes would intone) were in fortuitous balance above his grimy little head—he made one flawless execution of the required movements, with exact timing: bait laid into the dark water at the farthest length of pole and line; slow settling; minnow's hit and fisherman's smooth pull upward but a split instant apart; rise, release and subsequent arc of fish a portion of a draftsman's circle. For the time it took to happen I forgot in its beautiful perfection that its central actor, its geometrical pivot, was my little brother, or even that we were beings in time. He laid his pole in the yard as if he were a primitive ancestor laying his spear into the grasses of the plain, his body for a second frozen in the attitude of a sprinter starting; almost simultaneously the minnow hit the green, local lawn my grandfather mowed each week.

Luke grabbed the large peach tin we used to hold the snails, relieved it of its contents, and managed to trap the squirming minnow underneath.

"Measure it," he called to me.

No one ever issued a command more neatly combining imperious triumph with raw delight. He knew it was the biggest catch of either of our emergent careers.

So did I. A similar but more complex intuition also occurred to me. A little movie ran in my mind: I saw myself throwing the (his!) unmeasured minnow back in the bay, his screwed-up, tear-riven face presenting the details to our mother, her consequent look of *how-could-you?* aimed at me. Mercifully, the reel stopped short of the actual retribution her expression presaged. I had a choice of living that imagined sequence, or measuring the fish, and living with the aftermath of that.

It was seven-and-one-quarter inches long. Luke had no trouble holding it while I laid the ruler beside it. He gave me a look of pleasure and disdain such as a Renaissance prince might have given a friend whose unswerving loyalty he was about to reward with a beheading.

I had measured the fish. What happened afterwards I could balance off against the credit of having done my unselfish duty.

"I'll throw it back in," I said.

We wrestled a minute. When I had the minnow in hand I stood above Luke, straddling him.

"This looks like a good place," I said, lifting his belt as he tried to squirm away.

I pushed the fish into his underpants. He couldn't decide whether to run or resist and so was ineffective at either. I rubbed the fish through his shorts, feeling it slide against him. Duty had never been so adequately requited in the history of retaliation.

When I eventually let him go, he made a beeline for the house, pushing at his trophy until it finally eked from his pants and fell to the grass. He rounded the nearest of a pair of box bushes flanking the flagstone walk to the front door, and disappeared.

I picked up the minnow, a strange, drying creature which felt prickly in my hand, and walked to the breakwater, holding it out slightly in my upturned palm. It lay there, not dead—I knew this from certain implicit movements—but not unscathed either.

I knelt and let it slide back into the water. It floated up to the surface but did not show its belly. I felt an unexplainable relief. Slowly it began to move its tiny gills.

As it swam down out of my sight I couldn't help but wonder—my open palm still tickled by its delicate weight—if it would ever be the same again.

"I don't fish anymore," I said. "I don't enjoy it."

"Why not?" Luke asked.

"I have some theories," I said, "but nothing conclusive. Let's just say the hassle outweighs the rewards now."

We were in the kitchen of my one-bedroom apartment. Luke was paying me his annual twenty-four-hour visit, on his way back to Georgia from a sales convention in Pennsylvania. Plumbing supplies. Never far from water, my brother, whatever the circumstances. He always wanted to go fishing when he dropped by.

"Dry these, would you?" I asked.

Towel in hand and a clump of assorted restaurant utensils in the other, he leaned against the sink beside me. "What sort of theories?"

I dumped the dirty suds from the dishpan into the sink. A throaty *glug* rose from the drain; the water heaved and began to seep slowly out.

"Only one, really. It has to do with Daddy."

He laid the last fork on the formica countertop. None of its tines was parallel. "Some of your psychological shit?"

"Some of that. Yeah. Mostly." I sat at the table where we'd eaten our sausage and eggs, in his chair. I dried my hands, one finger at a time, deliberately. I watched my knuckles as if they had a secret message inside their incipient arthritis.

"Start with the dream," he said. "Isn't that what your theories usually start with?" He was smiling.

"Put the damn silverware in the drawer," I said. "The one on the left."

"Yes ma'am," he said, his smile broadening. "But only if you tell me your dream." This last came out in a broad parody of a European speaking bad English, Dracula in the suburbs.

"It's not much of one. I'm fly fishing a huge river. I hook something way out, about fifty yards, and start playing it. The rod bows. I see the sun glinting on the spot where the line enters the water. Then *I'm* in the water, under it, at that spot. I expect to see the fish I've hooked, or perhaps to *be* the fish, but I see instead a small, white, roundish piece of stone before me. It's translucent, pearl-like. Beautiful, but I feel queasy as I look at it. Then I'm back at the rod, fighting the fish again. When I land it it turns out to be the little white thing, sort of like the shiny part that seals a snail in its shell. It has a little knot of loose gristle sticking out on one side which I hadn't noticed before."

"And you woke up."

"No. I slept, but I remembered the dream the next morning."

"So how do you get from that to Daddy?"

I stood up and laid the towel on the counter. "Same circuitous route I always follow," I said. "You don't need to hear all that."

He spread his towel on the side of the sink where the utensils had been. The green of the counter showed through faintly where the wet parts adhered to it. We both leaned against the sink, staring at the vaguely beige wall across the table. Its paint flaked in a few places.

"OK," he said. "Just give the news."

"Well, the little white object with its hanging nugget of flesh ended up reminding me of the end of my penis when I was little. So the dream is 'about' my making my manhood my own—you know, catching it—and that usually means I'm trying to dissociate myself from Daddy. Using the fishing situation almost surely comes from his love of the sport."

We sat down, moving on cue as if we were dancers, except he swung his leg over the chair, cowboy style. I eased myself down, butt first.

"So you don't fish anymore because your dick's too small." It wasn't a question. He was looking at me across the table, not grinning. He seemed to be half serious, the attitude of attention, at least, being genuine.

I started to fiddle with the salt shaker. "Yeah," I said. "Bigger fish to fry than to catch." He smiled at that.

"I did oversimplify things, didn't I?" he said. "But you left me a big hole to fill in."

We guffawed at that one.

I rotated the little glass cylinder on its base, crunching a stray dot or two of spilled salt. It was difficult to lay the thin edge of the shaker precisely into the grain.

"That dream's three years old, in fact. It's taken that long for me to work things out. The long and short of it is"—smiles from both of us again—"I fished all those years not because I enjoyed it, but because I wanted to prove myself to Daddy, or prove to some shadowy audience in my head I could do what he could do." The reduction of so much frustration and pain to such a simple explanation struck me as miraculous, saying it aloud to Luke. It also sounded incomplete. I rested the salt shaker on the table and looked up at him.

"More than that, I was looking for a way to make him accept me. To hug me up to him, and josh with me the way he used to with his buddies." I looked down at the table. The salt shaker blurred slightly.

"He'd been dead ten years already, and I was still caught in that net."

Luke scraped his chair back and stood. He walked over to the sink and stared out the window. The leaves on the sugar maple had begun to turn. It looked like we were due a yellow autumn because of the lack of rain in August and September. The leaves would drop quickly.

He picked up his towel and held it around the back of his neck, rubbing himself gently with it.

"I know about that," he said. "Some." He let his head bow slowly, as if the pressure of the towel were bringing it down. "I've always loved fishing. Still do. Just for the feel of it—the water against my thighs wading, the seat in the skiff getting harder as the day goes by, the pull on the line, no matter how slight."

His voice kept the summer alive in it, yet there was a tremor, too, or the hint of one. He brought his head back up slowly.

"But I've realized for a long time it bothers me that I was always put in the small seat in the boat."

He dragged the towel down with one hand, laid it over the edge of the sink, and put his hands on it. He leaned forward and then eased his body out as if he were doing push-ups. He turned his head toward me.

"If you're satisfied with the kitchen work here, let's rig up and hit the river. OK? We can take my car this time. You don't have to wet a line, if you don't want to."

It wasn't a permission he was giving me, it was an acknowledgment. I accepted it.

"OK," I said.

On the way out the door he said, "You ought to have that drain looked at. Your pipes probably need a good reaming."

On the way to the James River—the roads were inversely proportional to their designations (11, 130, 608), diminishing in width and condition as their numbers grew—we told each other fish stories, a tradition we followed on these occasions. It didn't matter if we'd heard most of them before.

The windows were down. The morning sun, filtered by sycamore and ash and pine foliage, spattered the car, making it seem as if we drove through a medium other than air, denser, carrying its imprint as part of its elemental composition. Our words drifted into it, sometimes swirling, creatures with a life of their own as soon as we uttered them.

We parked in a cut-out next to the Norfolk-and-Western tracks, just past Gilmore Mills. The dust we raised on the three-quarter mile of dirt road behind us hung thickly as we pulled our equipment from his trunk and assembled and rigged the rods. To my surprise, he pulled out a new Daiwa spinning outfit, orange and black, with glossy black stitching at the line guides; it looked sleek and essential compared to my old eight-and-a-half-foot fly rod. I was almost ashamed to bring my antiquated reel out of the box: it was spring-loaded, with a retractable trigger you worked with your little finger. The design was supposed to release both hands for a better control of rod and line while you played your trophy, but it had become the signal of an inept fisherman, or one with reduced confidence. It was no longer manufactured.

Luke didn't even look at it. I was still fumbling with leader when he picked up his small tackle box and started up the fill and across the tracks.

I ended up fishing the near bank of the river for about a half hour. The feel of the rod as I cast was equivalent to riding in a big car— say an Impala—whose shocks are shot, and I had the sensation the tip was about to come loose. It didn't, of course. I laid the popping bug—smallmouth bass and bluegill populated the river in the fall—with some accuracy upstream under the overhang, but caught nothing.

The river was tea-colored, and not down as far as I expected, given the lack of rain. I waded out onto a graveled side bed and leaned my rod against a pile of faded driftwood the spring floods had left in their wake. Luke was downstream about twenty yards, two-thirds of the way across the river, which flowed slightly below his waist.

He was fishing downstream, letting his lure ride in the deep water just above a set of riffles.

Watching him, I warmed with admiration. I also thinned with it, seeing in his adeptness and savvy a reflection of my father's. He stood at a point where he had four vantages, equally likely to give him fish. He split two riffles downstream, the smaller on the far side of the river where he presently dangled his lure, the other, larger one on the near side, running wider and shallower, its head upstream a bit closer to him, and near enough to me to be fishable from the bank where I sat. Splitting the two riffles, a graded shelf pitched down into a four-foot cleft, making a V, itself a haven for tired feeders. If Luke turned around he had the far bank upstream, and the wide current at the center of the river as far as he could cast.

He worked the small arc of depth systematically, left to right, casting each time slightly farther up the bank shallows. I couldn't see the line come off his rod, but occasionally I caught the small splash as his lure hit the water. The repeated tableaus, subtly varied depending on direction and distance of each cast, made him resemble a magician waving a wand, drawing responses from the river's surface now and then: a figure from a medieval dream, isolate in the midst of primary forces, waist-deep in another element filled with life of a shape and design largely alien to his own, gesturing with a rod—an extension of his arm yet composed of material also alien to him and the creatures he signaled—seeking to elicit from them an acknowledgment, a connection. The line that would make such a connection tenable, even deadly, carried, because of its invisibility, the most magical dimension, as if what might be expected to break the image of dream in fact took it to a deeper layer of mystery.

He hooked something and began to work it. He turned slightly, and from the way he settled his body, getting a more secure footing, I could tell it was something big. He was doing his best to keep the fish from getting into the riffles, adding their surge to its actual weight. Apparently, since he had a short line out, this was difficult. I could hear the whine of the drag.

Luke began to work his way upstream and toward the bank, keeping the bowed rod at a 45-degree angle over the water. It was awkward maneuvering. He slipped on the rocks; at one spot the water deepened to his chest and he had to raise the rod above his head. Finally, finding solider footing in the knee-deep water, he seemed to have the fish under control. Then it leapt, breaking the surface for the first time, shimmying spume into the air, making with its body and the upward thrust of water behind it a dazzling curve of suspended motion and sunlight. It had to be a bass, perhaps one of the rare largemouth that fishermen would sometimes bring out of this river, but usually in the spring. This one looked to be three or four pounds.

Luke played it gingerly, yet my attention faded once the fish jumped and the engagement settled into its routine. Perhaps it was simply that I knew the procedure, that I didn't leave room for surprise, but I suspect it was more than that. Something at least to do with a vague sense of a superimposition of Luke over an image of my father, though I never saw my father wade a river, or manipulate a fly rod. But his ghost suggested itself, a spindrift of generation. He had, come to think of it, given me the rod and reel now abandoned among the debris behind me.

Saying *my attention faded,* too, isn't quite what happened, in the conventional sense of the phrase. My attention faded, yes, but as a scene in a motion picture fades, *into* another scene, complementary, reflective, inherent.

I was sitting on a boulder beside the pile of driftwood, the tea-colored river in Virginia before me with my brother stuck in it like a living stump; the far bank was lined with oaks changing to various shades of dull red and brown, interspersed with yellowing sycamores; behind them the midmorning sun turned the open field a uniform bright tan—all this *registered,* as we say, my perception moving outward, becoming more and more inclusive, seeking to enfold, finally, the farthest distance. But, at the same time, I wasn't there at all, as if I had become that distance.

I was floundering on a steep bank of the Connecticut River, somewhere north of Lee, Massachusetts. Also in October. A dreary, joint-stiffening drizzle rendered the dark, leaf-strewn ground slippery as a slug's belly. I shivered with cold. But I was fishing. I would have fished in any weather in those days, and did. Comparatively, I was mildly uncomfortable; the conditions for catching trout, however, were ideal: the river rising but not yet chaotic, and in the quickly diminishing twilight running roughly the color of the wet leaves underfoot.

At the instant of the memory's insertion between my present self and my brother, I had hooked something large and was trying not to let it drag me into the river. Swimming I do not like, even under the best conditions of clarity and warmth, and it was among the last alternatives I desired now. My feet twice slid out from under me, and I grabbed with my left hand for a sapling, holding the spinning rod at arm's length in my right, a tableau of a man in the posture of trying to keep his balance while sliding down a riverbank, having totally lost it. The atmosphere of parody, of inversion, extended beyond this flailing image, for it seemed the fish had me on the line, and not vice-versa.

With the help of the saplings, slick though they were with the rain, and the fortuitous condition of having unreeled only about twenty feet of line, I managed, in about ten minutes, to haul the fish out onto the leaves. I pulled it about fifteen feet up the bank, the corner of its lip hanging precariously from one of the treble hooks on the plastic minnow.

It was a gorgeous brown trout, easily twenty-four inches long, sleek and plump, glistening even in the near dark. I felt my heart racing more with the excitement of the catch than with the exertions that had accompanied it. I had begun already to imagine the drive back to my rented house, the gutted beauty on the drainboard, the story I would tell over and over to friends, its mellowing, rhythmic development down the years.

So I did the last thing I should have done. I lifted the trout and, settling it in the crook of my right arm, eased the hook from its lip. I neither slipped my thumb and forefinger through its mouth and gills, nor inserted there a pin of my stringer, hanging from a belt loop on my pants. I stood, a novice at the railings, holding in the tray of my hands two feet of compact, primal energy and experience only temporarily subdued, as if I were making an offering to the night and the river scouring it. The color of everything—leaves, the saplings' willowy trunks, the river, its opposite bank and the thin rim of sky above it, and, of course, the trout—merged into one opulent, surging umber, burnt and threnodic. My hands, pasty white, almost ghoulish, seemed to have intruded from another order of being. I remember not knowing for a second or two whose they were.

In that instant the trout moved, easily escaping my nonexistent grip. It flopped at an angle down the bank, the only direction it could have taken. I dove after it, in the ensuing desperate eternal minute recapturing it twice, holding it with both hands around its middle—once actually standing again—only to feel it squirt from my grasp each time. When it reentered the Connecticut I was calling "No. No." to the fish and the darkness, my voice making a broken counterpoint to the river's rush, filling the woods and my ears as if they were the world.

The slosh of boots leaving the current river and hitting the rocky side bed brought me back to my brother. I focused on him, or brought myself into view again—it amounted to much the same thing: he was soaked from the neck down, his blue work-shirt stuck to him, his khaki trousers loosing water into and over the sagging edges of his boots. Good humor washed his face, but the big bass I expected to see hanging from his fist on a stringer wasn't there.

"Where is it?" I asked.

"Where's what?"

"Your trophy. Your monster fish. Your Bass of basses."

He stopped in front of me, his legs slightly apart. He set the butt of his rod in the stones near his feet, balancing the tip against his outstretched arm so it angled away from his body. It was a version of parade rest. He tried to look puzzled.

"Come on, Luke. I saw you fighting it. I saw it jump."

"How long did you watch?"

"Not much longer after the jump." I kept my eyes on his with effort. "You'd started to work him upstream."

"Yeah," he said, replacing the fake expression with genuine plea-sure, almost glee. "Well, I lost it about the time you turned away. He threw the lure on the next jump. I never am sure how to handle those leaps—did it wrong again this time." No regret, however, not even a trace of chagrin, accompanied this admission.

"I have to admit I was distracted, though."

"By what?" I got to my feet and brushed the sand off the seat of my pants. My right foot was asleep.

"By the nude woman sunbathing in yonder field." Turning, he lifted his rod and pointed with it across the river. I couldn't see anything I hadn't already seen.

"It wasn't altogether shrewd fishing instinct that made me start taking that bass upstream."

I stared at him. My foot tingled a little, beginning to come back to life. When he turned toward me again something made me want to kick him with it.

"Hey," he said. "I got within a hundred yards of her. She's in a swale, spread out on a yellow blanket. You have to get practically up on the bank to see her." He brought the rod up so the tip pointed at my chest. "And a sight she is, at that. Worth a barrel or two of fish any day. Mermaid of the meadow"—I don't think his grin could have widened further—"except"—he did a little fencing jig and thrust the rod out closer to me—"she's got legs."

I shook *my* leg and began to walk up and down gingerly, looking at him once or twice; I also took a couple of glances at the sunlit field.

Luke walked over and leaned his rod beside mine. Then he sat down and started draining his boots. It was all very deliberate, though this registered on me only later, as if he were performing on land the sort of maneuvering he had done a half hour before on the far side of the river.

"I don't mind going back across," he said, retying his boot laces. "More than worth the trip." It was almost as though he were talking to himself. It may have been a soft sell, but when he looked up at me his eyes glinted with a trace of our father's impeccable mischief, which I had, at whatever age before his death, always been unprepared to appreciate.

I couldn't help smiling at him. "OK," I heard myself say. Whatever was going on, whatever routine he was playing out, whatever need was pestering him into making use of today's particular cluster of circumstances—whatever, in fact, he knew or didn't know about what he was doing, there was a nugget of good nature at its center and I gave myself to that.

Maybe it wasn't so much *good* nature as *our* nature, though I never have liked the sort of preconditioning that leads me to consider the two as opposites. In any event, I felt a relaxation of my reflexive distrust of my brother, as if spreading through me it became something else. Distrust thinned fades into acceptance, maybe, as the whole demeanor of the psyche changes when we drop to our sides the hands we have held up to ward off what we fear, or think we fear.

It didn't take us long to ford the river at the riffles below the cleft, and we made a comically quiet wade upstream to the spot where Luke thought we'd have the best vantage on his mermaid. There was a teenage furtiveness about the way we dragged our shins against the current, and as we rolled our bodies over the bank into the grass I felt, too, a vestige of the days when we played commandos in the park near our house. The suspicion that we were in the process of making fools of ourselves continued to nag at me nonetheless, and as I lay with my cheek against the ground, my legs cold from the water and already stiffening, I wished I were back on my side of the river sitting on the stones.

What *were* we doing? *Two* of us? Married, the fathers of four children between us, nearing the bogey of middle age. Was our aim now any different—beyond the obvious physical inconvenience—from opening *Playboy* to the centerfold? If it was—and it seemed to be; it *had* to be: there was a living woman in the field with us—well, if it was different, I didn't like to imagine what we would do next.

Take a peek and reford the river? I doubted it. But it was a little late for that, as for speculations about what sort of person the cartoon figure in our fantasies would turn out to be in the flesh.

I raised my cheek and craned my neck upward. Luke, to my surprise—and yet not—was twenty yards ahead, standing with his back to me. He did nothing to conceal himself; in fact, the composure and drift of his body suggested the opposite. Unabashed, he was about to make his move.

As if he knew by the tugging of an invisible wire stretched between us that I had surfaced, without looking at me he waved me forward. I stood, brushing myself off again, an empty gesture this time, since the front of my shirt was nearly as soaked as my pants, and the grit from the field where I had lain was part of its texture. I joined him at the drip line of the oaks and looked in the direction his pointing finger indicated.

"She's gone," he said.

The only interruption in the field's expanse of drying fall grass was a rectangle of yellow, presumably the woman's blanket, lying in a shallow dip some fifty feet farther on. We walked to it, Luke hanging back a little, mumbling about trouble with his left boot.

It was, of course, not a blanket at all, but the fireman's poncho Luke kept folded in his tackle box. Lying near its edge was the fish I had watched him hook and play: a handsome largemouth bass, probably upwards of three pounds, its green stripe, though dulled by being out of the water—close to an hour by now, I figured—still scintillant in the sun. It occasionally flared its gills, and once gave a small twitch of its tail.

I felt Luke draw up beside me, though out of reach. It would be a mistake to say he was tentative and I was angry; though the moment held between us a blend of such energy, it wasn't focused, or assigned.

"At least it's not in the center," I said.

"It's moved since I left it," he said. "I thought it might have flopped off into the grass."

The life of the fish—its beached instinct—separate from Luke's life and mine, brought to this crosshatched experience whatever obtained of conciliation, of goodwill, of mutual exchange. If Luke had expected an explosive climax—guffawing, rage, a wrestling match in the circle around the bass with all its attendant evocations of Cain and Abel and our own more recent primal tussles as young boys—he didn't get it. In my confusion of voyeuristic and inconsequential lust, and fear of what I might have had to face in my behavior once we'd confronted the woman I believed would be there—not to mention the relief I felt when she wasn't, and the positive affection I felt for the occasion of everything: this brave, sad fish—in all that confusion I was myself effectively neutralized, reduced to the matter of fact I was part of: my brother Luke and I at opposite ends of a sheet of yellow plastic, staring down at a three-pound largemouth bass.

He had caught it.

He was showing it off to his older brother.

I was leaning down and lifting it toward him, as he slipped a pin of his stringer through its gills and mouth, closing the loop.

Deep November.

Drear November.

The temperature was right at freezing and moisture poised on the bare tree limbs and twigs of the sycamores and poplars, hung at the edges of the sodden clusters of brown leaves the oaks would not drop until Spring growth ejected them.

It had been drizzling steadily for three days, was gray dusk at noon. Under foot the humus gave like a sponge.

In short—omitting other thorny, belittling environmental trivia—it was perfect weather for muskie fishing, the only time of the year they could be expected to bite, and Joe Skins—an old friend of mine who sold insurance—and I were taking advantage of this rare opportunity.

Since it was his aluminum johnboat we shivered in, our feet soaked from the trek through the woods to the river, and since he knew the procedures of catching muskie, he sat in the center seat, the fisherman. I sat in the stern, working the electric motor and guiding the boat, such as current and my stiffening fingers allowed.

We had spent the first hour or so coaxing eight bluegill and red-eye to take Rapalla minnows. We cut the larger ones up, and kept the three smallest in a bucket half full of river.

Joe had the last of these little teasers on his line when, near four o'clock, though it could have been dawn or doom's grim hour come round at last, he hooked something big. We debated as he fought the fish for thirty minutes or so, whether it might be a muskie, or a carp dumber than usual. It was clear after the first minute it was not a snag: it moved, and it moved deep and heavy.

"Muskie," Joe said. "Got to be. Carp don't lunge like that."

The drag on his Shakespeare growled again, a mechanical refrain for this struggle between man and leviathan.

"See? Carp just hang on your line mostly. When they pull, they pull down. Never have figured how they do that. It don't feel like they dive."

The fish stopped his run, a noticeably shorter distance each time now for about ten minutes, and Joe began to stir his reel again. The rod bowed, a classic tableau I never tire of, whatever the weather.

Which was, if anything, slightly improved. The drizzle had slackened and the overcast hung above us seemed a shade less bruised. It was as if the sky had opened a little to make room for whatever Joe Skins was, as the phrase goes, playing on his line.

The fish, to whom this routine couldn't have been play, finally exhausted itself. Joe reeled it in slowly, keeping the line taut; this final stretch of control seemed endless, but at last, about ten feet off the port side of the boat, we saw a long line of black dorsal slicing what had been the river's impenetrable darkness.

"Jeez," Joe Skins said.

"Yeah," I said.

Both our voices were hushed, as if the drizzle had lightened in order to assume their whispered sound. Until we spoke I had been aware only of the undifferentiated lumps, so to speak, of our immediate engagement with the muskie: the boat, two men, a length of line beginning with one of us and terminating out there at the invisible force in the water.

When we uttered our muted awe everything became very specific: I saw the rivets fastening Joe's seat to the hull, the paint flaking off the side next to his brown tackle box, squatting shut like a pet coffin in the eighth-inch of water filming the bottom, the laddered half of the black buckle hanging open at the top of Joe's left boot, a design repeated in the lizardlike skin at the back of his wide neck—a myriad of such details in and out of the boat, some intimate and some as impersonal as the mountains visible at the river's turning two miles downstream.

Besides the sight of the back of the muskie—for, indeed, that's what Joe Skins had hooked—what I recall most vividly—the image that comes unbeckoned, dragging with it all the others to which it is inevitably connected—is the black, plastic handle of Joe's reel, the little Phillips-head screw at the center of it shining its dimpled star at me—the only bright thing I saw the whole day—and Joe's hand, as if it were part of the handle and not manipulating it, so huge I seemed to see the star through a microscope instead of the curl of Joe's little finger. And I felt, too, that the relative size of Joe's hand—a ham to the stud of a clove—had brought that infinitesimal screw-head into existence, had given it birth.

I was for the instant I focused on that screw, and in all the instants of memory it has delivered to me over the ensuing years, as small myself—in that johnboat on the river in the mean weather surrounding me—as it was, and as ineffably, irreducibly specific.

When Joe drew the muskie alongside us, within my reach, everything reverted to the practical challenge of boating it. Most of that is a general blur to me, though I remember the stages.

There was no gaff in the boat, nor anything we could use as a substitute, so I tried first to lift it over the side. It was so thoroughly beaten it didn't twitch as I got it partway out of the water. I couldn't hold it, however, no matter where I placed my hands. It was too big, nearly four feet long and thick enough at its center to cut into steaks. After it slipped back into the water the third time, I tried the nets. Both of them, regular boat nets designed for fish maybe up to twenty-four inches. I knew one by itself wouldn't do; whichever end I didn't get into the net would be too heavy, and pull the rest out again. Joe was keeping the line tight, the bedraggled half of the bluegill he'd used for bait dangling about six inches above the hook still holding the membrane, visibly pulled, at one corner of the muskie's jaw. I put a net over each end of the fish and lifted, watching with increasing helplessness as it bowed, its center staying firmly in the water. Head and tail slipped out of the nets; I heard Joe call out something, missing the words but not the urgency of his voice—all hush and humility vanished from it—noticing simultaneously what he must have been yelling about: hanging from a cord of a net and no longer buried in the muskie's membrane was the raw, empty hook.

As if it knew the circumstances of its life had, for the second time in less than an hour, undergone a radical reversal, the fish undulated once, a sinuous motion in the water that produced its twin along my spine.

Joe dropped his rod. The two of us grappled for the muskie, only to feel it further awaken; the boat, too, no longer attached by Joe's line to the fish, began to separate from it.

We watched as the distance slowly widened. The fish repeated its supple unwinding twice more, and then, this time without seeming to move at all, disappeared.

Muskelunge.

I watched the dark, thin water close over where I had last seen it, becoming again a seamless depth, darker now with the muskie's withdrawal, as if it had incorporated a new shadow.

Though Joe and I were equally stunned, and deflated, losing a rare fish making us feel lost ourselves, aimless, it was different for me. It had been my fault. I lost the muskie.

We have remained amiable, Joe Skins and I, over the years since then, and I never labored my apology, or repeated it after he let me off that night at my front door. He has never referred to the experience, but after a couple trips back to that stretch of the James River the following spring, to catch bass and bluegill, we've not gone fishing together since.

My father and I sit together in the living room of his house. It's a Christmas morning like any other Christmas morning in my family until my twenty-first year. By then the planes of sadness and evasion had shifted perceptibly: our poses had become both deeper and thinner—which is to say habitual—and the tones of our desperate pretense had mostly lost touch with the needs out of which they had originally risen. But in the early years of this series those needs were still writhing, and the forms we groped for in which to embody them were not yet rigid and brittle.

My father sits in his wing chair at the far end of the room, diagonally down from the tree. I sit under it, or at the edge of it, tickled occasionally by the tinsel icicles and the bluish pine needles, trying at once to reach my presents and avoid bumping the ornaments from their bright hooks. We are at an enormous distance from each other: in the restricting space of the room we could not be farther apart; in my sense of his being in that chair— his few packages opened and their contents neatly stacked on the table beside him, his second or third bourbon cradled in his hand, his eyes wide with the energy it takes him not to look bewildered— everything is so diminished we could be separated by a continent.

That we share a common predicament comes to me in the image of our presents. He always gets a tie, and a shirt, and maybe a novelty item such as a set of coasters with roosters on them. Invariably I, too, receive clothing—let a coarse, woolen sweater with stylized stags in suspended progress across its chest stand as representative— along with a toy or some other frivolous object appropriate to my age. I hated the clothing. This was no gift. What relationship did a necessity have to a gift? My father appeared to me old and sedentary; what else could one give him but a vest or a pair of socks? And yet as I sat there, a continuing instance from my first Christmas to my last at my parents' house, I knew at some level that he and I shared a joylessness, or, more modestly, a disappointment we were disoriented by. He never grew past his; perhaps I have mine.

There was, then, no *play*, or a sense of the need for it. The heartrending thing is that neither he nor I was responsible for this situation. It was given us by his wife my mother, an environment projected from her constricted sensibility and spread before us like a great banquet of crusts and water. I was too young to know this, or contend with it except in the most inchoate ways; my father had been, and still was, too obedient a son to become an independent husband.

But I saw him be different, too.

One week a month he would travel on behalf of his budding (and later very successful) wholesale hardware and appliance company, dropping for six days his executive position in "the store" and becoming what he loved most to be, a salesman. Slipping into that mode was for him as easy as changing clothes, though it seemed not so much that he traded one set of lendings for another as that he *undressed*, showing himself openly in ways he was unable to do in the office. He seemed a different person, more amiable, quicker to laugh, and, from this distance at any rate, more vulnerable. He also drank less Kentucky straight bourbon whiskey.

Whenever the circumstances allowed, after I started school, I went with him on those selling trips—when holidays fell luckily in with this schedule, during the summers (even after I started playing city-league baseball and, later, coaching it), even in weeks when he could talk my mother into stretching two days off from school for teachers' meetings into five.

What made my accompanying him so acceptable to her under any condition—a matter of arrangement rather than permission— was that his selling route took him to Hampton; his "hotel" was his in-laws', my grandparents' house on a small bay contingent to Hampton Roads. Particularly in my sixth to tenth years, when I never spent a whole day with him or really wanted to, I'd go out in the morning or part of the afternoon to selected stores and then be a grandson in the big rooms until he turned up in the late evening, sagging but, usually, happy with his work, for a highball and supper.

In the early years I was aware mostly of a general tonality, an atmosphere of relaxation, of affability and shared concerns, and, in spite of his rigorous schedule, of a slower pace, or perhaps more accurately, of reduced pressure in his life. The men who ran the retail shops he visited seemed to welcome him in a way that encompassed more than their successful selling of the dependable, and therefore profitable, products he sold them. The commercial loop they took their places in, swelling the postwar economy while they restored their own material lives, vibrated with excitement. It was expansive and focused, national and local, at once.

Getting and spending it's called, pejoratively, by those who see themselves as spectators to its necessity, but for these men there was more to it. A glow of renewal rayed from them, warming even their most trivial talk, giving to words like *thermocoil* and *stovebolt* and *mattock helve* a human quality, as if they proceeded not just from the larynx and the tongue but from the bloodstream as well. They could be forgiven, in their headlong momentum forward, away from the terrors and deprivations of war, for neglecting their souls.

My father's part in this buoyed him personally, yet rendered him an anonymous cog in the larger enmeshings. I would watch him some mornings sipping coffee and inhaling a Chesterfield. Something about his eyes—abstracted, edged faintly by an unspecified worry—touched me as he looked across the room at nothing. He picked a fleck of tobacco from his tongue. Then he would focus and resume reading the newspaper, or look at me and smile. I never knew if such instants were signs of the diminishing insecurity and fear with which the war—now over five years behind us—had undone him so often, of if they signaled a deeper understanding circumstance was incidental to, that, war or not, he couldn't count on anything he loved or sold or otherwise gave himself to, to sustain him, or, itself, to last.

This, of course, implies I had, at the time, a way of embodying my germinating and fleeting intuitions. I didn't. At best I sensed a fissure beneath the solid, confident surface of his behavior on our trips, and that sensation weighed little in my daily involvement with him. As I say, he seemed personally more than his job to me when he was doing his job, and I thought the same valuation showed in his associates' responses to him when he entered their stores and spread open on their polished oak counters his monolithic catalogue.

It was on that formidable hulk—it could not be called a document, or volume, or a tome, for it outweighed and outbulked any such reference: a current mail-order brochure that bears the label *catalogue* is the merest onionskin hint of a page in my father's embodied Platonic Catalogue. Set on its end, last page against the table, first page a skyscraper of stories above it which, unless it was spread for the search of an item, was its usual *status quo*—it rose at its slimmest—after my father had culled obsolete entries, say—to a height of fourteen inches. Its supple and battered leather front and back measured fourteen by ten, to protect the reams of standard pages stacked between them. When my father would "open" it— that is, unscrew the caps and lift some portion of that stack—the stainless-steel rods their double perforations encircled would rise into the air above his desk like columns on the Parthenon. If his catalogue had been set on a shelf like a normal book—which, of course, it never was—it would have taken seven copies of the Jerusalem Bible, spine by spine, to equal the space it occupied.

It was on that formidable hulk that my initiation into a more intimate knowledge of my father's selling life depended. When I was big enough to lift it, to put my hands around its two leather handles, muffed by a three-inch leather collar that fastened with two snaps, and carry it from the car into a store, and, an hour or so later, back again, I had passed some barrier whose existence, until I passed it, I had not suspected.

I can still feel it, the first time, bumping my shins as I carried it in front of me with two hands. I got it to the glassed double doors of Fenwick's Furniture Company and my father, in a sort of relay, carried it the rest of the way in. After a while I could take it to the counter by myself.

"Hey, Seth," Mr. Fenwick would call out as my father held the door for me. "You paying Mark enough for that work? Wouldn't want the unions on your back."

Then he'd greet me as if somehow I were part of their routine now, included in the ritual banter of entrance and exit, procession and recession.

Mr. Fenwick would haul the catalogue up and set it beside the cash register with a thud. "Wow, let me feel that bicep," he'd say, or "I wouldn't want to tangle with this one in a dark alley."

During my last two years of grammar school, when I made trips with him, my father enacted the charade of being dependent on me for the portage of his catalogue. In spring and early fall, when the spot or shad or croaker were plentiful, my new level of intimacy meant I went on fishing trips my father's customers arranged for him.

It had been Mr. Fenwick, in fact, who had suggested it, one day adding what amounted to an invitation to his usual cliché greeting.

"A boy who can heft this thing might be a good fisherman, too," he'd said. "What do you think, Mark? A five-pound shad'd be easy compared to your dad's refrigerators."

I said, "Sure," without thinking, or rather *with* thinking, for the image of those shadow-weight minnows aloft on their way to my grandfather's lawn popped into my head as I spoke. I wasn't as certain as I so abruptly sounded.

By way of nods and smiles my father and he agreed to take me along on their next outing. It was only years later, long after I had gone mostly into my separate life, that they included me in their poker games, the other activity that constituted the social parts of Seth's escapes to the seaborne freedom of Tidewater.

Mr. Fenwick's Chris Craft—low and sleek, with glossy red doors covering the inboards—literally took my breath away. He would steer with one hand, half the time his head turned toward my father, yelling, and I would be both exhilarated and scared we'd run into something—a buoy, another boat driven by someone as casual as Mr. Fenwick, one of the great gray ships bulking in the evening sky across the Roads from us at Norfolk.

They gave me a bait-casting rig, so I didn't have to confront too early the inflexible stretch of a boat rod. I had handled one, apprehensively, the night before in my grandfather's garage, and had realized if they set me up with that I would have very soon become an unwelcome annoyance.

I don't think I caught anything—maybe a couple of small croaker —but it didn't matter. What did was being with my father, seeing this man—for whom the only complexity he could speak clearly about was the merchandise he sold, who had only the grossest lexical markers through which to express his perplexing emotional life— become articulate. It was not a verbal articulation, but one of the whole personality finding itself, its outlet and extension, in gesture and activity.

His stubby fingers, usually so dry he had to lick them to turn the pages of his catalogue, baited a hook as delicately as a pastry chef's edging a cake. He fileted the smaller fish we kept—mostly spot—in as few motions as it takes to fold a letter and slip it into an envelope. His compact, already sedentary body—five-feet seven, 155 pounds—became a gymnast's, casting as if he were manipulating a wand instead of the unwieldy boat rod, turning in the confines of the seat as if he were performing on a stage. He spotted his casts exactly. His forefinger against the rough line barely touched it, as sensitive to the fish's deep curiosity as a guitarist fretting an arpeggio.

Whereas the others—I am moving now from the four of us in Mr. Fenwick's cruiser that first trip to any boat, large or small, anytime during this roughly two-year period, so that these observations become representative—would "horse" the fish's bite to hook it, my father Seth Random would seem barely to give his rod an upward tug, yet he would land more fish by day's end than anyone else.

It was not the numbers, however, that impressed me, nor were they the center of the others' obvious admiration of and pleasure in my father's presence. He was first a whole man, given to this circumscribed pursuit with seriousness and skill and good humor, a guide who unwittingly brought us all away from the frayed, anxious disorder of the rest of our lives and showed us what human involvement could be—play and absorption, measurably purposeful, communicative and mysterious at once, full of the unknown and power and surprise as the awful water obscured it, yet accessible, too, in the form of the complex life that could be lifted from it in sport and, later, taken again in nourishment. He showed us that limits need not coerce or confine, but rather could focus and set free.

This was my submerged feeling, heartened by the uncomfortable love of the man I didn't know how to feel or express, and so became the crux of the experience for me, radiant into my future self in ways that I learned both limited and released *me.* I doubt if any of his cronies ever worried those trips to such an interpretive length. For them—my second category here—he was, simply, good company.

"Seth, you remember, don't you, how hard it was to get help?"

"Oh yeah. There wasn't any money to hire anyone with."

"You got that right."

"We had one darkie who stayed with us—I mean literally: slept inside the loading dock on a palette through the whole thing. He took whatever we could scrape up at the end of the week."

"We had guys show up at the door all day. You could see them get skinnier as the months went by. I got so I stopped looking at their faces."

"There were times I thought we'd all end up in the street. God, I was crazy. It was like living in a jug."

They were talking about the Great Depression—five businessmen in their forties and fifties burning the undying past, and branding it even more deeply into their memories with each breath.

Bill Talliaferro had anchored his cabin cruiser in the mouth of the Chesapeake Bay; they fished for whatever the ebb might carry past them, the boat with its assembly of friends forged in the same furnace a dot in the gray expanse of water. I wondered, feeling so cut off from everything here, what it would be like on the Atlantic.

"Hell," Art Tignor said, "millions of people *did* live in a jug. I had three uncles who only drank a couple beers on the weekends before the Crash, wind up alcoholics. One of 'em made his own, even though they repealed Prohibition before the worst of it hit my family."

"Thank God for Roosevelt." Bart Fenwick was the only Democrat in the boat. Nobody seemed to hold it against him; in fact, he afforded a counterpoint they all enjoyed.

"Roosevelt, shit. The only thing he did was make sure we got into the war. *That's* what started to change things."

"Seth's got that right." This was Bill Talliaferro's refrain. His bushy mustache, concealing his lips, seemed a sign of his verbal inactivity. Since so few words emerged from his mouth, the overgrowth had no friction to hold it back. Everyone else in the group shaved every day.

"Goddam. Looky here, will you." Mel (a nickname, short not for Melvin but for Mellifluous, because of his voice, a stroking of velvet) Rooney's rod bowed nearly double, then straightened as he lowered his hands and began to reel.

"Don't rough him," Fenwick said.

"Looks good, looks good," Tignor murmured, almost to himself. Sitting at the wheel, he took a long pull on the bottle he had collared in a brown bag.

My father kept jigging his bait, but watched Rooney's struggle on his left. I stopped slicing up the small fish they all had been saving for bait, letting my hands rest on the top of the cooler I was using as a cutting board.

As Mel Rooney's engagement lengthened and became routine the excitement thinned, as if an electric current had passed among everyone—except, perhaps, Bill Talliaferro, who hadn't interrupted his huddled attention to the line he had out over the stern—and subsided, leaving us mildly stunned.

No one spoke for a while. I listened to the screech of Rooney's drag alternate with the slow rush of his wet line curling on the reel, the irregular slap of water against the hull, the snip of my knife against the cooler top.

Seth Random leaned forward and rested his elbows on the wide gunwale. He let his line slacken, its motion on the bottom determined not by his control of the rod but by the dip and rise of the boat. He turned his head and, seeing me watching, winked. Then he lowered his head for a minute. A fitful breeze ruffled his thick, graying hair, and beyond him the overcast sky darkened at the distant horizon, smudging the line it usually cut at the treetops on the shore.

Rooney boated his six-pound sea trout with little difficulty, everyone centering on it, envious and pleased for its captor, until he slid it in the catch box with the smaller croaker and bass swimming there.

"What's he doing in here, I wonder?" Rooney said.

"Some of them leak in here out of the Atlantic," my father said. "I've heard big bonito have been taken up in the Maryland end."

"Fish are dumb," said Tignor. "I don't care how smart they are."

The conversation ebbed and flowed, recalling other catches on other outings, veering now and then to women. Sexual innuendo flew over my head, but I think I realized even then how they avoided direct expression on that subject, being evasive and euphemistic, as if tiptoeing around something in the middle of the floor it was either too frightening or too fascinating to look at.

They told jokes, mostly dirty of course, as the talk afforded context for them. One I remember, which I heard again recently, can serve as a sample.

A madame at a brothel—they would have said "cathouse"— heard the doorbell ring one evening. She opened the door and at first saw no one on the porch. Then she spied a man, all four of whose limbs had been amputated, plopped on the floor. "What in the world do you want?" she asked, sneering. "I rang your doorbell, didn't I?" he replied.

Their laughter wasn't forced exactly—Fenwick rarely responded at all—but it seemed circumscribed, defined by its sudden demarcations, a clipping on and off of sound. It seemed as though an undertow of attention, noticed vaguely if at all but no less constant for that, had found a sound but not a voice. It reminded me of my father's way of turning the tuning knob on the radio when he knew the program he wanted: he would flip past other stations so fast all you could hear was the abrupt blurp of their presence on the dial, and then they were gone. Something complex and extended in time was going on at each of those tiny red lines, but there was no way to find out what without letting the tuner rest there.

None of those men chose that kind of patience with the deeper, unsettled currents of their lives, accepting instead the noises rising from the displacement and reduction of what passed for humor. It was another dimension of what made me uncomfortable in their presence, and yet, at the same time, I sensed in the uniformity of their routines something established long before they were born to their parts in it, a compromise, almost instinctive, with forces too immense and subtly intertwined to be faced head-on. They were hostages to themselves, so to speak, as small and isolate individually in time as the group of us were in that boat, idly rocking on the floorless waters of the Chesapeake Bay.

I loved them in this awful setting, but most of all my father among the acquaintances who admired and accepted him in ways no one in my family, including me, seemed able to do. His wink, and his bowed head, became a moment of discovery for me, if not of a dimension of consideration in the man himself, then as a projection of my own need outward into him, so that the two of us, so different and distant in character and generation, were, in a more ancestral, impersonal family, kind, and kin.

That kinship surfaced in places more unlikely than Bart Fenwick's Chris Craft. My father ritually brought home, at the end of his selling weeks in Tidewater, pound tins of backfin meat from Chesapeake Bay blue crabs, and of shrimp—cooked, peeled, and "deveined" (another euphemism I still respond to affectionately when I hear it). He distributed them among his three brothers, who all resided with their families within a mile of each other, and of their parents, on the north side of the city where we lived. When I accompanied him, he'd take me to Hartog's Crab and Seafood to buy these gifts.

Stuck on a dangerous curve on the busy, two-lane road across the neck of one of our bay's sub-inlets, Hartog's presented an unpromising front to the traffic speeding by it: a long, once-white veneer of plasterlike gunk spread across its one-story, cinder-block wall. The whitewash and plaster both peeled incessantly, a changing pattern of surface decay, like a leper's skin. Two windows, laid in horizontally near the flat roofline, broke this flocculence with their gray, dirt-encrusted rectangles.

Perhaps because it was a wholesale establishment, Hartog's presented its best front not to those who passed it on land. On the water side it was immaculately kept, regularly painted (not whitewashed), scrubbed down with hoses and long-handled brushes wielded from the dock where its boats tied up. Leopold Hartog vonHohenfels cared only for word-of-mouth that moved over water, as if birds crisscrossing messages against the twilight.

Inside, rows of women, mostly black (*darkies* was my father's word for them), faced each other on either side of tables set end to end the length of the room, as if for a gigantic harvest feast. They shelled the crabs, peeled the shrimp. Periodically a man would pass through and pick up the deep trays the ready meat was heaped on, carrying them to the packers out of sight in another such room elbowed on pilings out over the water at the back of the building.

No one seemed to be working in any particular hurry, so my eye was never overcome by a preexistent confusion when we opened the door to the room, and entered under the jangle of the cowbell mounted above it.

While my father transacted his business with Leo Hartog, or whoever was manning the retail counter stuck in the corner behind the door, I would watch the women pick crabmeat. Their hands worked without haste, but with unvarying rhythm. These hands appeared to me to be independent creatures—their adept fingers like the claws on living crabs I had seen performing subtle manipulations—for the women never seemed to be paying attention to what they were doing. The long room, shaped like a wide railroad car, bore the rise and fall of their conversations as waves undulate a buoy, and that slow, almost dreamlike sound complemented the intricate shuttling of their hands.

Between the women the trays of succulent white crabmeat, or plump, gray shrimp, rested beside the inedible detritus piled haphazardly on spread newsprint. I never saw a scrap of the meat so much as tilt over the side of a tray, but from the piles of shell pieces slid to the benches and the floor, so the trays became odd islands of impeccability in an ocean of debris.

Similarly, the women's hands—we usually came in during the end of the day shift; Hartog's was a twenty-four-hour operation— always looked as if they'd just been washed, but their butchers' aprons were, as my mother might have put it, an unholy mess. These contrasts occurring intimately together mirrored the two exterior fronts of the enterprise.

Though I wasn't confused, I was, during my youngest years, set aside by our stops at the seafood works. It was as if the intrusion my father and I made there was a reciprocal one, the activity and the environment—so integral and circumscribed—interrupting the boundaries of my life, themselves no better formed than the new shell of a molting crab. I would slip my hand inside my father's and hold whatever part of it I could get a purchase on. When he needed both hands to pay the cashier, I'd grab a handful of his trousers. Though his habit in most situations was to rebuff my clinging, in Hartog's he accepted it; sometimes I would feel in his hands a kind of nervous search, as if my smaller ones weren't quite sufficient for his need to hold something for support.

He was outwardly affable with whoever waited on him, and he would greet and say good-bye to the women on the benches nearest the front, but his voice took on the mannered joviality of the stereotypical salesman I heard him use only rarely in his work, with strangers he was calling on for the first time, or with the few customers with whom, beyond their commercial interests, he had little in common. This bothered me in those contexts, but in Hartog's it brought me a measure of security.

I have no external, visual record of such moments between my father and myself, but a photograph from those years—somewhere between my fifth and seventh, I guess—shows my grandfather and me holding hands. We are on the wide sidewalk of Queen Street, downtown, perhaps in front of Woolworth's where I would later buy my *Daredevil* comic books, which I preferred over *Batman* and *Green Lantern*, for instance, because they featured more writing. He's nearer the plate-glass window, fobbed up in a three-piece suit that's off the rack but looks as if a tailor fitted him for it. It appears in the black-and-white print to be a light brown or tan herringbone. He has mounted his stick-pin—a crab centered by a tiny diamond— just below the dimple of his four-in-hand. Hatless, his stunning bald head picks up a glint of the sunlight angling against the base of the storefront.

I'm dressed in a sort of informal wool coat, the kind of apparel my mother would have called *elegant*, open in front, flared at the edge below my knees, a miniature tie and vest, long pants underneath, and a short-billed, round cap digging into my crown, anticipating the curve of bangs on my forehead.

We both smile, whether for the camera or because any other expression would destroy the unity of the pose, it's hard to tell. His hand meets my hand so our arms create a flattened V from his shoulder to mine, an odd visual effect of combined awkwardness and relaxation. Sideways to the building we face down the street, as if ready for whatever might cross the bridge and emerge toward us around the bend. Our reflection is perfectly reproduced in the plate glass, as much exchanged satisfaction between each other implicit there as in the illusion of substantial bodies in the photograph itself. In spite of the discomfort the restrictions of our suits must have caused us, we clearly had overcome it, and were touching at a level our exterior trappings had nothing to do with.

My father's and my hands joined imperfectly in Hartog's are a version of that photo, the center of interdependent vitality and emotion in the midst of a somewhat more unsettled tableau.

As they were again when he was confined to a hospital bed, at sixty-five, with lung debility, the first crisis his emphysema visited on him.

His doctors had assured my mother he was dying, in and out of a coma, or something resembling a coma, hallucinating, and dangerous to himself in his spasmodic attempts to jerk the oxygen tube from his nostril. My mother had refused to have his arms strapped to the bed rails, preferring to commit herself, and members of his brothers' families, to a constant watch beside him. I canceled the few conferences I had scheduled for the week and drove up to take my turn, and do whatever else I could to help.

I came also, I thought, to say good-bye. Or to live through it. As it turned out, though the doctors believed the walls of his lungs were composed more of cigarette tar than of tissue—as a brick wall may eventually be supported by the ivy that has beriddled its mortar—he survived the attack. But for three or four days he played footsie with Dolly Death—or Doris, or Delilah, as his alliterative whim dictated in subsequent accounts of the experience, not always as lighthearted as he tried to make them.

I sat with him through the night of the third day, my chair facing the bed and the window beyond it, my knees prodding the lower edge of his mattress. Occasionally I had to grab his hand before he could take hold of the oxygen tube, and help him turn when he indicated by his grunts and the twitches of his shoulders and hips that he wanted to change position. Since the head of his bed was elevated somewhat he never rested long on either side.

At first, at the initial movement, I rested my hand on his so he wasn't able to raise it much above the sheet. It was like two odd, five-limbed creatures wrestling with each other. But later, out of boredom and curiosity, and to prolong active moments to help myself stay awake, I let him almost touch the tube before I intervened. This caused more energetic struggles; his emaciated arm, bared by the loose sleeve of his pajamas luffing toward his shoulder, was stronger than it looked. Giving him such leeway also revealed multiple causes for his movement: twice he took a deep drag on an imaginary cigarette and removed it, once tapping ashes off it in the air, the other time offering it to me, turning his hand delicately so the burning end pointed toward him. He looked past me, his eyes deeply blank, but when I shook my head he reversed the aim of the cigarette and brought it to his mouth again.

He adjusted his glasses, raising his eyebrows in assistance as the tip of his finger touched the bridge of his nose. He scratched his bristly cheek. Once, smiling, he tipped his hat, his head lifting slightly from the pillow.

For the most part he slept quietly, but now and then his dreams erupted into speech.

"That's a handful," clearly pleased him and seemed hooked, as a couple of adjacent remarks helped me infer, into a party at which he was the center of attention: "I can get under *that* bridge," and then something about "old knees yet" and "best in the bathtub."

"You remember, don't you?" he asked once, fluttering his fingers vaguely toward me. His eyes were closed; he was dreaming again, but I replied anyhow.

"Remember what?"

"We loaded the whole car before it was over."

"Yes," I said, and paused. "Before what was over?"

"The war. You remember."

"Yes," I lied, "I remember. How did you load the whole car?" I thought it must be a railroad freight car he referred to; there had been sidings on each end of his old warehouse.

"Willy helped." His forehead tightened, deepening the furrows normally grooved there. "And Russell. And all the old ladies." Some tears started down his cheeks. "All over. They came from all over. They brought their fans." His weeping stopped as abruptly as it had begun. "They waved at the bombs." His mouth became a taut line across his face. "They threw the dollies at the bombs." His voice rose, a wiry keening. "A waste, you wasted it all."

I succeeded in calming him, but the dream persisted. He mumbled unintelligibly, and then said, "If they save all the pieces they can try again. Tell Cary, you hear? Tell Cary."

"Tell her what?" I tried to keep it going, or to participate in its going, but this time he didn't seem to hear; no dovetailing occurred and I never learned what he wanted me to tell his dead mother. He fell silent. Pretty soon his body and face visibly relaxed, and his lips flibbered with his shallow breathing.

Toward dawn I was dozing, my forehead resting on his bed rail, my arms poking through it, splayed on his covers. A movement of his arm—or a muscle asserting itself in his arm—woke me. I raised my head to find his eyes open. We looked at each other as if everything were normal, as if we were talking opposite each other over coffee and sweet rolls, about to begin just another day. I wanted to ask him why he had that silly pipe stuck up his nose.

He repeated the flexing that had awakened me. He wanted to lift his arm. I withdrew my left arm, but before I could get the right one off the bed he clasped my fingers awkwardly against his palm. Following the signals his movements passed to me, I shifted sideways in my chair until we were holding hands in a mild imitation of arm wrestlers, his forearm raised to allow us to entwine thumbs.

His grip was firm, but I felt no desperation or panic in it. I tried to return the pressure equally, continuing to take my cues from him.

His eyes encompassed me, drew me together, as a lens focuses light into a single, intense point. I cannot, of course, measure the time that passed while this occurred; sometimes I believe it was *my* dream I remember in the early morning, that the experience never occurred outside my wish for something like it to happen as part of my vigil. I had, after all, not slept much during the night, and had suppressed for some days under myriad trivialities my anxiety for his life.

Still, I recall it now as involving both of us, drawn out of our mutual sleep, alert in that little room where daylight through the cracked blinds had begun to lay its soft bars against the ceiling. That interstice in time, and in the hallucinatory drift and slide of his illness, ended with a few words, spoken clearly to me, with warmth and what he had garnered of love from our generally inarticulate years together.

"Looks like I'm the one in the boat now," he said.

Then he was asleep again, gone off—though I didn't know it at the moment—to a qualified recovery.

I held his limp hand a few seconds longer before I lowered it to the sheet.

In the Christmas mornings of his living room I watch him—the same tableau receding down the years as in a row of mirrors—take a sip of whiskey, three short fingers and thumb holding the glass, little finger cocked out and down, lips slightly parted and pursed, tongue curled to greet the rim. He places the tumbler back in its coaster with the deliberateness that is one signal among many of his incipient drunkenness. I recede involuntarily within—my own series of reflections joining his—grief-stricken, angry with him for removing himself this way from our shared condition as counters in my mother's holiday manipulation, and with myself for expecting, again, that it might be different this time.

I dreamed of our someday being allies in this war, of his refusing the bourbon, taking instead into his hand my hand and saying, "Come on, Mark, let's you and me get out of this place today. Maybe we can find a different kind of adventure." He never enacted this comic-book scenario, and I never fully expunged it from my consciousness, or the less accessible nets of my mind.

His brothers and their wives arrive serially over the next half hour, duck into the living room to say hello to me and ogle this year's version of the ideal tree. Soon they are all in the dining room having their annual breakfast of oysters, ham, and a repulsive gruel called hot-water bread. The undifferentiated din of their conversation rises and falls as I sit on the floor and piddle with my gifts or, as the scene flips year to year, tend to Luke, or read, sometimes sitting in my father's vacated chair.

My mother's "You can find something"—waving at the gifts and wrapping paper scattered about—"to amuse yourself with while we grown-ups eat," anchored me there. She meant to be humorous, but a thin edge of sarcasm betrayed itself. She never said, "Play with yourself," but the overtone of that unconscious invitation lay in the air like a smoker's last, faint exhalation.

My lifelong impulse, no matter where I am, to be somewhere else and to have my father with me, may have had its inception on these mornings. If it didn't begin here, as is likely for an urge so primary in its strength, then these mornings helped codify it. I owe to them also my first suspicions that my last name was more than a sound labeling generations of a family, that it might somehow have an appropriateness verging—paradoxically, given its meaning—on determination, that, indeed, it tied me into my own fate as neatly as a clove hitch around its cleat secures a boat.

"Pass the potatoes, please." My grandfather's voice, though modulated for family dinner, retained some of the imperative tone he used in his office for the more recalcitrant agents and secretaries who worked for him.

"Got some gravy you don't want to waste?" my father asked.

"Oh, I'll waist it, don't worry about that." My grandfather loved a good straight man, and my father loved to oblige him. It was one of their standard little schticks. "A waist is a terrible thing to mind" was one of their favorite, Spooner-like reversals, long before the American Negro College Fund's television ads, and an athletic wag's subsequent parody of their slogan.

"Why don't you two work up a new routine?" My grandmother's fork made a slight *tink* as she laid it on her plate. "You could use some of that time you sit in your boats, watching the tide change."

"That's not all we watch, Maud," my grandfather said. I imagined he glanced quickly at my father, sitting to his right at the cherry dinner table, lengthened, as usual, by two leaves for our visit. My empty chair sat at an angle to the table next to my father, and my grandmother opposite my grandfather at the head (or foot; neither was ever specified). My mother and Luke, in his high chair, completed the oval on the long side across from Seth and me, going counterclockwise.

"We keep real busy. I've mounted a searchlight on the bow of the bateau, and I always carry a pair of waterproof binoculars over my shoulder. I wouldn't want to miss any stray pair of bloomers."

"Russell, not again."

"Why not? It must have been a wonderful sight, Paulette Amicord's lacy understuff streaming in the wind."

It was, as my grandmother's demur indicated, an old story. The experience itself didn't move my grandfather to repeat it, as much as the fact that he'd missed it and had to take a back seat when his friends who'd been there rehearsed, and enhanced, the details.

Paulette had been on her sailboat with a "beau" (as my grandmother labeled such male hangers-about). They had become becalmed on their way into her dock, without paddles, and to add all the cloth they could to catch the smallest breaths of breeze, the two of them had rigged an auxiliary sail out of clothes—his shirt and her bloomers. An unexpected gust of wind, so the story went, had capsized the overmasted vessel.

"When Paulette finally hauled her bloomers in they were full of fish," my grandfather concluded.

"Her bloomers are always full of fish." My father got the punch line this time. The two women performed on cue their hushed and sudden intakes of breath.

"Daddy," my mother whispered. "Little pitchers." That was one of her favorite shorthand signals to avoid certain aspects of reality, as ineffective as the rest, like telling me a few years later that the used condoms floating by the breakwater were balloons from a party. Sometimes she flirted with the truth in spite of herself.

"Where *is* Mark, anyhow?" my grandfather asked.

"In the boat," my father said. "Way out to sea by this time. He's probably too far to make it back by dessert."

In the boat meant *under the table.* I shifted my body, curling a little more tightly around the twin center posts supporting the table's frame.

My conception of where I was confounded the elements; I saw myself as captain of this static ship, yet under water as well. It was no submarine: I was on water and under it at once, the ship a convenience only for the surface. The locations were not consecutive, but simultaneous. I could breathe anything. If the ship caught fire, an attractive possibility, I could handle the flames, too.

My sea was populated by the legs of chairs and by other people's feet. My grandfathers' heavy wing-tips differed from my father's only in color, the one black, the other brown. My mother, too, wore a version of her mother's thick-heeled white ankle-tops with white laces, only hers were a classy tan intended to give elegance to the overall effect, a color I suppose designed to change *shoes* to *footwear*. All it did, however, was create a slightly unequal dowdiness. Luke's little sockbound feet, banging against the rail of his high chair up near the skirt of the table, didn't count as far as my marine universe was concerned.

These feet performed all the movements feet have invented. They crossed casually at the ankle, they poured directly into the rug with the same inertia as the chair legs, they bent outward, first one and then the other, at the ankle like an awkward adolescent in mid-heat, they stretched forward trying to dislodge me from my bridge, they scuffed, they fidgeted, they tilted their toe skyward, and, reversing the pivot, did miniature *pas de deux*. When my father sometimes wore loafers or slippers—nights he got home in time to soak his feet before dinner—he would push each one off and spend ecstatic moments scratching the instep of one foot with the big toe of the other.

I would imagine this array of shoes as characters on my vessel, ordering them about, observing their discomfort before my gaze, steelier than Long John Silver's, deciding which would walk the plank this time for mutiny. Or I would transform them into fish, schooling them skillfully into my net or fighting one of them for hours in the rolling Atlantic waves off exotic Florida.

What fascinated me most, however, was the change the whole environment suffered when the maid, Delia, came into the dining room to serve a new load of fresh beet greens or sliced beef, or to collect dishes and bring whatever came next. Her version of the two seated women's shoes were down-at-heels, with a growth protruding from the upper of one of them, encased in a thick, transparent stocking in better shape, I thought, than the shoe. The growth looked like a little creature poking out of its lair; perhaps because of its rough, reticulate texture, or its flaky dryness, I could never imagine it as living under the sea. The tops of her stockings had been rolled down to her ankles, forming a kind of barrier there, giving her lower extremity the look of having been added in a factory.

All this would have unsettled me if I hadn't known Delia to be the gentlest, best-humored person in the house, the only one besides my grandfather who communicated to me an instinctive acceptance. Whatever complex expectations, and therefore judgments, I was internalizing in those early years of my life—or had already internalized, erecting my own prosecutor, judge and executioner for the long trial ahead—when I entered the kitchen while Delia was hulling limas or peeling spuds, or accompanied her on her slow, floppy walks around the garden when she had a moment to herself, I felt them fall away, like bean hulls and potato skins sliding from the plate into the garbage bucket.

She laughed a lot, a low, rumbling chuckle in her chest, the aftermath of which would hum in her throat and emerge from her lips more like a song than laughter. Her dark skin, often filmed with sweat in the kitchen whatever the season, came to carry for me associations of richness and depth, not so much because of the pigmentation—though that was indispensable—as the open nature of the person it enveloped.

When I was older, and she was older, I drove us to a nearby pick-your-own strawberry farm one spring to get berries for a dinner party my grandparents were giving some old friends. It may have been a family reunion. Luke may have accompanied us—it would have fit the division of labor that week—but if so I have expunged him from the memory.

Delia and I worked on either side of the rows of plants, leapfrogging each other as one of us exhausted a section. Most of the time our hands were some feet apart under the thick leaves, but occasionally one of us would close in on the one ahead, and for a moment we would be next to each other. Once or twice, as if choreographed, our hands—her black, arthritic knuckles disfigured by the protuberances the disease had wrought; my uncalloused, pale fingers for all the world like underwater flowers drifting in the current—turned the lush, burgundy-colored fruit skyward in complementary motion, and picked four or five or six berries, dropping them simultaneously into the small cloth sack on the ground beside us.

Occasionally she'd look into the bag, noting the increasing height of the strawberry pile inside it, and say, "That's picking some berries, Mark."

"Yes," I'd say. "Can't beat us, Deely."

"Good team, un-hunh," she'd hum, and the few syllables would again be music in the loam-scented air.

"Un-hunh. They'd go a long way to do it better than we be doing it."

Her feet moving around the edge of the table, inserting themselves between the chairs at either end of the oval, flicking behind the legs of the chairs as she passed from one person to another, created a queasy sense of undersea, or oversea, dislocation. It resembled the effect of a carnival ride stopping, hanging suspended, its motion transferred abruptly to the crowd around it.

I would bear this, fascinated by it as I have said, drawn illogically to the slight, increasing seasick feeling in my chest, somehow connecting it with Delia herself, the rest of whose body and person I couldn't see but whom I imagined with a sharpness of feature and contour I never experienced when I imagined the rest of my family in their chairs. It was as if Delia were a sorceress holding us enthralled in the magic line she drew slowly around the table, yet because of my curled body's diminutive repetition of that oval and my concentration at its center—because of my invisibility, too—I alone had a chance to escape the spell, to join her beyond its rim.

It always became more than I could manage. I would close my eyes. I would rest. I would begin to becomemyself.

"What's for dessert, anyway?" My grandfather, a European immigrant, was unfashionably alert to dietary matters, heavily favoring fresh fruits and vegetables—raw cauliflower was a panacea of his—but when it came to desserts he lapsed as radically as a Bavarian sybarite.

"Delia," my grandmother called. "Bring the cake, would you?"

"Too bad Mark's gone off," Granddad said.

"He's not a cake eater, though," my grandmother said. I watched her slide her napkin out of her lap and beckon me with a crooked finger.

"That's true," my father said, "but I recall he's been partial to black forest in the past."

Delia's feet eased in between my father's and Granddad's. I heard the cake platter nestle against the metal trivet.

I watched her withdraw and turn, following her legs and feet until she disappeared around the room divider. The sound of her footsteps on the linoleum of the runway between the dining room and the kitchen lingered in my ears as I crawled out of my seaship kingdom and resumed my place at the table.

I had come to the farm in the New River Valley of Virginia to visit my grandmother's cousins, Katharine and Louisa, 80 and 68 years old respectively. It was a retreat of sorts during the summer before I went off to graduate school, and, as it turned out, got married the first time.

For the two weeks of unseasonably fine weather—which they remarked on in wonder and puzzlement daily, as if what felt like a blessing might be otherwise—they took care of me as if I were a celebrity they were preparing for a special appearance, a benefit performance or an award.

Though the farm no longer produced anything except their basic needs from a small garden beyond the barn, they set out breakfasts fit for a crew of regular hands. Plates of sausage patties and fried ham and crisp bacon made a triangle in the middle of the linen-covered dining table. There was toast—white and wheat—a rack of muffins, and a tumble of biscuits rolled in a napkin and nestled in an oval basket. Scattered about were jars of orange marmalade, homemade strawberry, peach, and black-raspberry preserves, and a small silver bowl, sweating from the cold of the refrigerator from which it had been recently lifted, filled with a faceted mound of quince jelly.

And eggs. Scrambled on a blue-flowered serving platter, fried—both sunny side up and over easy—on a plain one; boiled and still hot in one basket, boiled and cold in another.

We feasted, and afterwards the two old hogs in the pen beside the shed did, too.

The days themselves were filled with long walks, and longer stretches of quiet during which Katharine and I read, and Louisa tended to chores about the house, mostly invented, as fictitious as the novels with which I occupied myself. We drove about the county to visit friends and relatives so distant as to be themselves fictitious, about whom and whose kin in turn I heard stories and more stories, impossible to track in the telling much less remember.

One of them, knowing I was going to graduate school, tested me, asking me to guess the acreage of his bluegill pond. Another wanted me to explain to her why the mountains were blue, had they always been so. A boy three or four years younger than I, rawboned and sour of expression, brought me a bag of cherries he'd picked for my departure; when I went to eat them I came on three stinkbugs, nearly biting into one.

Our meals in the evenings were as Spartan as our breakfasts were opulent: cold sausage and biscuits and a sliced peach; a salad of spinach and lettuce with some tomato wedges and a shredding of ground ham; strawberries and cold chicken pulled from the bone, my favorite. And tea, steeped so long it could have been poured in the corner and formed a stalagmite.

This apparent schizophrenia derived not from any complex dietary or ritual preoccupation, but from a simple division of labor. Louisa fixed breakfast, Katharine fixed supper. Their specific attention to me was even more accidental. Katharine was silent and withdrawn for most of the morning, so Louisa bore the entire responsibility for conversation at breakfast. After supper, however, Louisa "retired," with a degree of ceremony, to her bedroom next to the kitchen, eventually to compose her plump but compact self on the feather tick for the night. Katharine and I established very quickly a habit of sitting together on the front porch.

It was unscreened so we had bugs—she called them "peskies"—to brush away. Because it faced east, we couldn't watch the sunset, but we were variously intent on the delicate phases of the fading of its light on the long vista of grass crossed in the distance first by the dirt road into the farm, and then by the ridges of those blue mountains rising into the gathering dusk.

She kept a little stack of books on the large hourglass-shaped wicker table beside her rocker. She read to me from Sappho, and Horace, and

George Herbert, making small hmms and giving gentle intakes of breath that seemed after a while a kind of punctuation that made the rhythm of her engagement inseparable from the rhythm of the verse itself. Her voice thinned slightly when she read aloud, which struck me as grating at first, but I came to be grateful for the absence of a throaty, or breathy, or otherwise theatrically excessive rendering of the lines, which I realized I had expected from an elderly woman. Her voice was clean and only far enough removed from its everyday timbre to suggest the words she read were an ordering of experience more intense and remarkable than daily speech. That slight distance seemed, I thought later, to suggest that the basic difference between poetry and our daily presentation of ourselves in language was one of pace, of elongation in time, as if daily speech were lacking only a consistent compression to focus, as poetry does, into an audible form we can immediately recognize.

She also read books on contemporary physics, and would occasionally ask me to interpret a paragraph or a sentence, or to respond to an idea. She was fascinated by the growing attention paid to the relationship of the two hemispheres of the brain to each other.

"I never did hold with calling somebody deep," she said once. "A well's deep, and the ocean, and I can accept deep blue. But the figure of speech just won't transfer to people, do you think?" She tilted her head toward me slightly. I nodded, not wanting to interrupt where she might follow this thread.

She turned back to the meadow—if, indeed, she was looking at it— and patted one of the volumes lying open on the table. "Or to literature, either," she said. She picked up the book, closed it, and held it up toward the mountains, its spine level with the horizon, as if she were taking a sighting on something. "How can you call that deep? And a single page is about the thinnest item in the universe this side of air."

She liked imagining electric impulses traveling through the corpus collosum, and the wonder of memory and time. One of her figures for memory was radiance, each of us a wheel of experience at the center of which, ever intensifying, the mind seized and released what it made itself of, relinquishment as crucial as retention in its composing and recomposing.

"The mind is a dendritic spangle," she read, "a concert of chemical and neural activity one of whose central mysteries is only by convenience

called memory." She latched onto the phrase "dendritic spangle" for the rest of my stay, saying it with delight at odd moments, not quite a mantra.

"How big is our brain, anyway?" she asked one evening.

"Oh, I don't know. About the size of a quart jar, but not shaped that way, I guess." I said. "Give or take, depending on the person."

"House of time," she said. "You know, I can imagine someone of George Herbert's time"—she tapped a volume beside her that may have contained his poems—"thinking of Scripture as a building, bigger and more complicated than any cathedral it was preached in. You with me?"

"Yes."

"Full of closets and secret panels that led to whole worlds of surprises. Thoughts. Contradictions."

"Yes," I said. "I can see that."

"Well, our mind's bigger than the outside world we live in, too. Like Scripture to the cathedral. And memory's like Scripture in the preacher's mind."

The dispersal of light across the paling timothy, its drifting in the irregular breeze, the hazed mountain range seeming to shift somewhat through the refractory distance, and the small intimacy of the two of us on the porch with our books and separate thoughts, untimed and improvident, all took on the dimension of her understanding for a moment, became infused with it as with breath, and I could feel mind moving over the blowing grass as it is said to move on the face of the waters.

Neither of my children cares about fishing. Or fish, either, in general, though they both like salmon grilled with butter in a Cajun smoker. My daughter, who lives in Maine, will also eat fresh lobster (but not Florida crayfish) though I think it's less for the lobster than for the drawn butter and lemon juice she dips it in.

Her hair, which she keeps short, is roughly the color of that mixture. It's rich and thick, and approaches an aura that would become a second head, so to speak, if she didn't get it cut regularly. She is sensitive about such proportions: her hazel eyes are large, her breasts small, and she tends to be slew-footed when she's inattentive. I don't know anyone else who is more striking to see or know. She is vivacious enough for three people. When she was little I used to look in on her late at night; even though she was as still as moonlight, I had the impression she was an energetic sleeper, working deeply in her dreams to keep her life there full and eclectic, too.

It's ironic that she's settled in a small town near the coast of a state for which fishing has been a necessity and an emblem since the early decades of the country. Her spirit is as far from hooks and sinkers and nets as the Gorton's ad depicting the man in the yellow slicker is from the daily life of a trawler operator in the North Atlantic. A second irony inheres in her running a card and oddments shop, an indoor life for a woman who once loved to run and dance, and sleep under the stars. Once she spent the deepest part of the Alaskan winter in an Airstream trailer, tending sled dogs for an Iditerod racer.

She still runs in the evenings sometimes, and hikes the Appalachian Trail with friends in New Hampshire during summer weekends, but these blurts of activity seem mostly vestiges of her habits when she was younger. There was a period when I hoped she might take up a career with the forest service, or create for herself an indispensable niche in an environmental group, but the bureaucratic organization and political infighting ran her off early.

"Besides, it's getting to be all computers," she'd said one evening in her early twenties, visiting me in the North Carolina mountains. "You don't get outdoors all that much. The days of the weather-seasoned forest ranger keeping up the line shacks and being at one with the wilderness are over. All that's been reduced to Smokey the Bear."

She was bustling around the kitchen of the house I was renting then, putting together a homemade pizza, already a specialty of hers. The sauce simmered on an eye of the cook top, the debris from its making scattered about the butcher-block island and the counter beside the sink—shreds of garlic paper, the greenish outside peel of an onion, green and orange pepper seeds, snowflake-shaped splatters of tomato paste. The detritus of a minor storm.

"It's 'forest management' now, with the accent on management. Timber thinning, bond issues, policing the tourists. What you have to put up with from the Winnebago crowd is incredible."

She seemed to take these disappointing insights out on the cheese she was grating. Her right elbow rose a little higher on the backswing and she bore down on the grater as if it might take a notion to fly away.

"You're going to bend that thing," I said.

"What?" She looked up at me, her eyes wide and focused inward. Then she came to herself. "Oh, this." She straightened, staring first at the grater set over the small bowl the cheese wormed into, and then at the little nub of mozzarella in her other hand. "Yeah. I tend to get carried away."

The conversation drifted here and there, and by the time we had finished eating she'd asked me how I was getting along. Those were her words—*getting along*—which made me think of the "little doggies" of the old song, and then the suggestion of aging, neither of which associations I expect she knew of, much less intended.

"I'm getting along," I said, imagining a sprightly calf cavorting along a dotted line toward a billboard cutout of an old bull put out to pasture. Knowing she wanted more, I added some comments about the consulting business being good. I was, in fact, being asked to do more jobs than I could decently accept. It was July, and the dreadnought of the reopening of schools wasn't far off. Teachers' groups—mostly localities in the state—were seeking help with curricula, discipline, and other unending sources of consternation. Even the most cut-and-dried principals were admitting things were falling apart and couldn't be handled internally.

"No," she said. "I meant how is your *life*. You're rattling around in this huge old house"—she extended her arm toward the ceiling and rotated her hand on her wrist, her forefinger inscribing a circle, the others curled toward her thumb: it was a dancer's gesture—"sleeping on that palette in the corner upstairs. And not eating enough, right?"

She picked a piece of pepperoni from the leftover pizza and laid it on her tongue like a wafer. Over her chewing she said, "Not that it's such a bad house. I loved the way the sun colored my walls this afternoon."

I gave her a little time to launch into an elaboration about my diet, and diet in general, but she finished the pepperoni in silence, and reached for another piece.

"Go on and eat the whole thing," I said.

She smiled at the pizza and picked up the slice she'd been denuding. "Well?" she said, looking at me again as she took a bite. "You happy, or what? Anybody you want me to meet?"

Mischief and shrewdness mixed just about equally in her tone. I was a little unsettled by the way she reversed our places—daughter checking out father's love life—but at the same time I enjoyed her doing it consciously, and enjoying herself, testing to see what she could get away with, yet, more seriously, wanting us to begin to know each other as man and woman. Or so I thought. It wasn't comfortable, as I say, but real opportunity never is.

"I don't think about that—the being happy, I mean. If that happens, it happens. But I am involved with my life, not just my work but the person I am doing it, watching myself doing it." I don't think about myself in these terms much, so I sounded awkward, an amalgam of talk-show jargon, pop psych, and simple ignorance. It didn't, however, seem to bother Morgan. Maybe it sounded normal to her.

"I'm not absorbed in anything. Or anyone." She cut her eyes at me over the slice of pizza she was about to take another bite of, and smiled, her eyes glistening with doubt.

"True," I said to her expression, but I was more interested in pursuing the distinction that had occurred to me. "That might be what happiness could be, for me anyhow—absorption in something, the slipping of self into destiny." My own words surprised me.

"You talk funny sometimes," Morgan said.

"Your brother the reader says I talk like a Victorian novel."

"Half brother," she said. It wasn't her neutral tone by itself that tilted our immediate engagement toward another depth at this point, but the beat she skipped before she spoke. She put the butt of her slice of pizza on the plate and eased her chair out behind her. From the table across the kitchen to the sink she kept her head slightly bowed, her eyes presumably on the pan she carried.

Her back to me, she began to transfer the scraps to a piece of foil. Her motions were deliberate, differing from the intensity with which she had grated the cheese, as if she were willing an ease she was incapable of achieving. I noticed her stocky calves below her navy blue culottes; they reminded me of my aunts', and my father's mother's. Morgan would have the same difficulty keeping her weight down when she hit middle age. When she turned fifty I would be seventy-eight, which meant that right now—midsummer of her twenty-third year—I was still more than twice her age. Through the haze of these discomfiting numbers I stared at her, cleaning up, but no longer saw her. Suddenly she could have been anybody. Or nobody.

We had named her Morgan after her maternal grandfather in spite of my reservation at the double trochee: Morgan Random. Not as tripping as Malachi Mulligan—her brother Martin had pointed that out when he first read unreadable *Ulysses* as a senior in high school—and perhaps therefore, to my ear anyhow, somewhat blunt, as if someone were halted abruptly in the midst of falling down stairs. But, with a literary person in the house, other associations beyond her grandfather inevitably crept in. For a while she was Henry Morgan, the famous Caribbean-based pirate, until Martin's Camelot period, when she became Morgan le Fay, the infamous sorceress, Arthur's half sister and temptress of the Knights of the Round Table, the mother of twisted plots and all things murky and sinuous with evil.

When she learned a "fey" was a fairy she had shielded herself against the name, bickering with Martin and retreating into pouts when he used it, hating the Tinkerbell definition she thought it trapped her in. But when Martin, mistakenly thinking he would upset her further, told her about some of the Arthurian Morgan's rarer escapades, she took to the name like a fish to water.

The complex pattern of sudden reaction was apparently still active: a seething hush surrounded her as she walked by me on her way upstairs. Yet I hardly noticed, to be frank, I was so absorbed in memories of her.

A flickering set of images at first, hardly more than subliminal, hooked together probably by their shared tonality of sadness and regret: in the laundry sink, at six, fully dressed, scrubbing herself with a cake of Lava, as the water flowed over the edge and into the basement storm drain; at some point in her ageless infancy singing to the mobile of rainbow fish, stirring slowly in her breath, suspended above her crib; at ten—the year her mother and I separated—bent over the edge of the creek at the bottom of the hill, pulling the legs off a small frog, her face streaked with slime and mud.

As this little kaleidoscope spun out its mergings I moved my eyes from the door through which she had passed to the photograph of her that sat on a shelf of the corner cabinet beside it. This seemed an unconscious shifting, but who is to say that the force of memory hadn't turned me to include the full-color image of Morgan standing on the prow of a sailboat, holding with a raised hand a guywire that disappeared at the photo's top edge? Holding the sky in place? The pose and location belonged to her late teens in New England, when she and I had come to the farthest stretch of our estrangement. I knew nothing of her life during this period.

In fact, the last time we had seen each other—excepting her high-school graduation before that photograph was taken—had been almost ten years ago this month. I had moved here with Martin—now a senior away at Cornell—after the divorce, given up the bookstore I managed in Winchester, and had begun to inch toward a living that might seem more independent, at least of the strictures of the retail trade. I had met a local teacher at a literary soiree and that brief, inaugural flirtation had led to my first "consultation" assignment as well. I had made more than I should have of my tutoring in college. By the time Morgan arrived for her first official visit, my new routines were under way. At least I could present myself to her as if I were more settled than I was. Facades, then, were *my* specialty.

Except for fishing, which was where I lived. I went during most of my spare time—that is, most of my time—committing to memory the network of hairpin, rutted back roads that led to remote native trout streams, or the upper reaches of larger rivers, overgrown and rarely fished except by the devout and the desperate, into both of which spiritual categories I fit. The fisherman who is absorbed by his pursuit, and by the larger tapestry in the whole of which his threaded image is subsumed, learns—has netted within him—the places where he goes, where his activity unfolds. I, on the other hand, knew how to get *to* those places; the tracks of the journey were gridded in my dreams. But once at a given spot I became a thrash of loose wires, a spray, my attention suddenly without focus, my perceptions rendered opaque and unmemorable by an interior release of emotions, as if a nictitating membrane had been pulled over my open eyes. This happened whatever the exterior circumstances.

They were legion. And I was at their mercy. It seemed to rain often, or to be unseasonably hot, or buggy. I would be molested by shoes that suddenly were too small, or too large, by a sweater that was drawn magnetically to the hooks I fumbled with, by undergrowth that parted before me only to snag the handle of my reel, or the small bait box I carried on a string over my shoulder, or my rod tip, or my frayed temper, which itself became palpable at one point or another on almost every trip. I was a rage in the thickets, and in the streams themselves I spent two-thirds of my energy keeping my balance on the loose and uneven rocks. The rest of it I frittered away retrieving my spinner from twigs and branches and, occasionally, my L. L. Bean pork-pie hat.

Even in the midst of it I knew it was comic, but I rarely laughed. Sometimes, having slipped and concluded a teetering progress along a stream bank by sliding into the water as if into second base, I would give in and cry. A grown man, yes. It was mostly cerebral weeping, though, its cause held within the immediate details of the scene I watched myself inhabit, never spreading inward to the distortion and loneliness and bewilderment that drove me into the wilderness in the first place.

Morgan arrived, by bus, a Monday morning after an especially haggard weekend from which, despite a repetition of the chaotic routines I loosed on the woods and waters of Haywood County, I had brought home two smallmouth bass not really big enough to keep but, at a pound each, trophies to feast on, for me.

When she stopped at the base of the bus steps, I saw her and thought a lyric sentence simultaneously: her hair's still curly and her eyes are still blue. The first of these details, I learned, was the result of some new home salon treatment, and would straighten again *(Ugh!)* in time; the sunlight caused the second, slanting against her hazel eyes in such a way as to lighten and simplify them. They regained their chameleonic subtlety as I moved to hug her to me. Her head, turned sideways, fit into my sternum, and through my cotton sweater I felt her arms placed tentatively against my waist.

We had four days together.

Breakfasts at IHOP, one day at the zoo, another walking the streets downtown—peering into the big windows, getting snacks at forbidden hours, going to a movie in the afternoon—parts of others hanging out in my apartment where she read romance novels (*Wuthering Heights* the oldest), the fashion and comic sections of the newspaper, and the Yellow Pages. We had tea and scones from the bakery downstairs, where the pet parrot, whom I had never known to speak, called out as we entered and left, "Good parts. Hard parts," in a furtive, sharp-edged squeak. Some of the high-school teachers were involved in a summer institute, so we had lunch one day with them in the cafeteria. Monica Summers, who had helped me arrange my first consultation session, took Morgan to the gym and the art rooms, which excited her; we went home for her to change clothes. I was astonished at how agile she was on the exercise mat, nearly double-jointed in her rib bends, and like an acrobat with her flips and kips. She stayed most of the afternoon. Monica ate dinner with us, I remember. She and Morgan talked about dance and art programs at their schools, making a little island with their conversation.

Four days, buffered, over almost before they'd begun. On the last afternoon I took her to Lake Walker.

I rowed the metal johnboat out into the center of the lake. Morgan, wearing a ratty T-shirt over her bathing suit, sat in the stern seat, my tackle box on the bottom between us. She wiggled her toes at me through the rents in her sneakers.

"Those things come that way?" I asked. "A fashion statement?"

"Not exactly. But they're meant for you to cut holes in them. Why are you stopping?"

I shipped the oars. "So we can fish. The breeze'll push us toward shore. When we get in close I'll row some more to keep us from tangling in the bushes."

I handed her the better of the two spinning rods that had been lying angled over the bow seat, like splayed sprits. "Do you know how to cast one of these?"

"Sure, Dad. I learned from my *Field Astream* video." She grimaced at me, and then smiled. "I've only tried this once, a year ago in New Hampshire, and I didn't catch on then."

"OK," I said. "Sorry." I let the mistake with the magazine title go.

It took her about five minutes to get the knack of letting the line slip off her finger at the right instant. The water was deep enough so if she retrieved her spinner too slowly she wouldn't hang up on anything. We sat there awhile, a plausible imitation of two old hands, silently flipping out and reeling in. Around us the loblolly and white pines soughed occasionally, and red-winged blackbirds kept vigil on the scrub growth on the banks nearest us. In twenty minutes I had four nice hand-sized bluegill; Morgan hadn't had a bite.

I manipulated the boat so she was casting in the area where my fish had hit, but she still drew a blank.

Eventually she stopped casting and stared at the rod, then at the oarlock, then at the water. Sweat glistened on her shoulders and upper lip.

"Would it ruin things for you if I went swimming?" She bopped— there was no other word for it—her head toward me, her eyebrows slightly raised. I felt for an instant as if we were caught in a parody of a TV family show.

"No, of course not," I lied, as she peeled off her T-shirt. "But slip off the back there. You could probably dive OK, but supposedly there's no swimming outside those markers"—I motioned toward the shore where we'd put in. "No use calling attention to ourselves. Stay on this side of the boat."

She said, "OK," sliding into the water; she took a few breast strokes, surface-dived and disappeared.

She swam with the same ease and dexterity she'd shown in the gym, equally adept at all the strokes, shifting from one to the other as if she were fulfilling a privately choreographed aquacade. In the midst of a crawl she would suddenly curve downward, a bowling ball sinking, and reappear doing the back stroke in the opposite direction, pushing off the end of some imaginary pool. Her series of single-stroke rolls from crawl to backstroke sometimes were dizzying, her body becoming rounded lengthwise in the water she pulled with her, suggesting a porpoise. Her body seemed to have

produced an oil that made her sleek and released in her a fluidity
of motion and energy.

The three or four fish my desultory casting produced over the next
half hour I absentmindedly added to the stringer hanging from the
bow ring. I noticed it was full eventually, letting it slide back into
the water. When I looked up I couldn't find Morgan.

It was one of those thriller movie scenes, I told myself to diminish my incipient anxiety, where the swimmer stays under beyond
credible limits and the person in the boat feels time pass like lava,
its mass and viscosity a weight in the chest. But she didn't come up;
I put down the rod and started to unbutton my shirt, noticing even
as I did what an absurd gesture I was making. I heard what seemed
to be a faint rattling sound but couldn't locate it.

She finally surfaced, of course, with a turmoil of water and air
whooshing around her, right in front of me, grabbing my hat with
one hand and the gunwale with the other. I leaned backward from
the shock of life shooting out of the water, and nearly fell over the
other side of the boat.

"Got your pork chop," Morgan said, holding the hat scrunched
up in her hand like some parody trophy.

Levering herself with her hand on the gunwale, she bounced up
and down in the water as if she were on a pogo stick. The boat
rocked. I grabbed the seat and held on to it until she released me
and things settled down.

She backed off about ten feet, drenching my hat. Then she did a
push shot off the top of her head, arcing the soggy chunk into the
boat. It landed square on the tackle box.

"Two points with the old man's pork chop," she called and as
quickly as she had broken from underwater she became still again,
not even visibly treading water.

The sudden quiet seemed momentarily to freeze and heighten
everything: my hands still holding the seat on either side of me,
knuckles pale; the tackle box, a sick, seaweed green under the tan,
shapeless blotch of my hat; my copper-colored rod angled against
the aluminum stern seat, itself a sheen of brightness, a flat plane
cut out of the surface of the lake, a deeper metallic blue against it;
and beyond that, hung into the water as if by a marionette's crutch

from the sky, Morgan, her blond hair flattened to the contour of her skull, expressionless—upward daughter, downward fish—a person buoyant in her separateness from me, yet so deeply a part of my unknown life that if she drowned I would drown with her.

It was from some depth of that kind I seemed with effort to raise myself now, seeing again the photograph that appeared, for an instant in my recovering it, black and white. Then Morgan's deep-blue bathing suit etched itself once more into the lighter background blues of sea and sky. Her hand on the guywire might have been waving to me.

I nodded and stood up, rubbing my right knee. The Random aunts had been troubled with arthritis, too.

In the hall on the way upstairs I passed my line of fly and spinning rods—none of them rigged—leaning against the open stone. This house had originally been an inn, two centuries ago, and over the years no one had added closets. Two tackle boxes, a nest of nets, and other assorted equipment sat on the floor in the angle the rod handles made with the wall. My father's knife—a clever device consisting of two wooden handles, one of which had a cavity into which the blade of the other fit, a sword into its scabbard—protruded from behind one of the tackle boxes.

I climbed the stairs and, seeing her light pooling in the hall, quietly stationed myself in the doorway to the room Morgan was using. She was seated at the kneehole desk, writing, her back still to me. She seemed totally absorbed, made smaller by her withdrawal from the rest of the world. I was surprised when she spoke.

"It's OK," she said. "I'm almost done." She continued writing as she talked. "I keep this journal not so much as a record as an outlet. My private therapy."

She held her pen out to the right, tilted her head, and appeared to decide something about her current entry. "I've filled maybe thirty pads over the last couple of years, but I've never gone back and read anything I've written."

She put the pen down. "At first I thought that was stupid, but I realized the expression's what matters. If there's anything I need to go back to, I figure I'll remember it." She closed the journal. "Or recreate it. I've read that they're mostly the same process."

Before she had a chance to shift in her seat, I asked her, as noncommittally as I could, "Were you writing something about Martin?"

"No," she said. "Not this time. I was putting down a dream from the other night."

She turned the chair and resettled her compact body in it. "Want to hear it?"

"Sure." I went over to the bed and sat at the end of it, pushing aside an old quilt my grandmother had made.

"I'm in a field of magenta and purple flowers, about waist high. Lupines, I think. At least they reminded me of the lupines I've seen in New Hampshire. They extend endlessly in almost every direction. I'm so full of them—their fragrance, their color, their *presence*—it's like I'm one of them. I browse my hands back and forth over the ones I can reach and the whole field waves, like grain in the movies, only it seems they're an ocean—I guess that's where 'waves of grain' comes from, only these weren't amber. It's a communication among us, too, like we're waving *to* each other. It's a whole world." She paused, clearly immersed in the vision again.

"But I said *almost* every direction on purpose, because from the beginning I'm aware of not looking off to my left. I'm not afraid, or don't think I am. It's more like a pressure keeps my eyes from turning that way. So part of my action is wanting to look but not wanting to, at the same time.

"Then, as part of the movement of my hands over the waving lupines, my gaze swings to the blank direction and off in the distance, on a little hill, so far away it seems minute, like a background detail in a painting, I see a house. It's a frame house, painted brown—or the world is naturally a dark color—with turrets and curved porches, complicated and very old. It feels, well, warm—"

She cut herself off here and looked at me. "You sure this isn't boring you? I get so involved when I write in that journal"—she nudged with an elbow toward the pad lying on the desk beside her—"I forget how weird some of it would sound to anyone else."

"No," I said. "Go on. It's fascinating." It was. I was drawn into that field, and toward that house.

"Well, if you say so. The house feels warm and I want somehow to be there, but I don't want to give up the field of flowers, the extension of me all around me. But I guess the house is, too—an extension, I mean. What I want is for the house to enfold me and my field, and somehow not enclose the space and the outdoors of everything.

"Nothing changes, though, except a person comes out onto one of the porches and waves. Or I think he—it's a man, young—waves. He could be adjusting some hanging basket of flowers, or changing a light bulb, but he could also be waving.

"The thing is I don't have to wave back. All I have to do is keep moving my hands across the tops of the lupines and my response travels on them to the house, right up to the edge of the porch where the boy is standing."

She stopped, gazing at the corner of the room to my left. Her voice softened, but became more distant as well. "It was like what I sometimes think a miracle could be. Just as normal as anything else, presented, you know. Given. With no la-de-da."

"Do you try to figure out dreams like that?"

She snapped her eyes to me. "No. I don't tamper with them. When I remember them, which isn't all that often." She reached around and picked up the pen. She began clicking the point out and in.

I got up and walked to the bookshelf opposite. "Do you see your mother much?" I pulled a volume halfway out, and then eased it back in.

"Not all that much. Some." She diddled with the pen. "Hardly at all these last three years, actually." She looked at me quickly again. "Marvin's taken her to Portland, did you know that?"

"No," I said. Marvin was her husband of four years.

"I don't read her letters. Just pop the pudgy little envelopes into the old Glad double-cinch." She tossed the pen back on the desk and sighed as she stood up, as if she'd expended great labor, or was done with something. Or something indefinite but unavoidable was beginning.

"You remember when we went fishing?" I asked her. "Last time you were here?"

She laughed. "Yeah, I remember turning all your fish loose while you thought I was drowning. I thought sure you'd hear that chain rattling while I unhooked all those oversized safety pins. Boy, the expression on your face when you pulled that empty chain out of the water."

"Glad I didn't disappoint you, " I said over my shoulder.

"You couldn't figure it out, could you? Really."

"Not for a while. Then I couldn't figure out why you'd done it." I started to turn and face her, but I didn't. My right foot pulled slightly against the throw rug.

"Well, it wasn't ecological, I can tell you that," she said.

"Maybe," I said. I let my finger slide down the spine of a book, looking away from the case past the desk and at the window panes framing the darkness. "You seemed like a fish yourself that afternoon."

I could feel her stillness near the doorway, like her self-possession when I first came upon her at the desk, writing.

"Field of fish," she said, her voice a settling of sound in the air. "Field of fish."

Then, startling me, she was rubbing my right shoulder blade, gently.

Then she was gone.

My son Martin, eight years older than his half sister, was more clumsily overt in his one attempt to participate in what seemed to him my weird need: to entice fish to engage me on the other end of an indeterminate length of monofilament.

He was sixteen, I think, home in late April for one of what seemed a plethora of breaks at his prep school. The proportion of in-session to holiday time made it seem as if the study periods were breaks from the weeks of time-off. Then I envied the teachers all those vacations, and said so to Martin; now, having seen firsthand the bedraggled and harassed teachers in the various systems I visit, I know how hard-pressed they really are, how nearly impossible most of their jobs can be and how little time and energy they have for the real work they originally hired on to do: teach their subjects.

Martin would deflect my objections by talking about how much he loved the place, and how great the people were. In truth, he had, after a couple of weeks of rending homesickness (which at my end I mirrored), blossomed at Mt. Southfield, beginning to fulfill the indications of independence and ingenuity he had shown since his mother's death forced him out of his childhood when he was five. He not only made A's, he learned things, and made what he read part of the way he approached his life.

He called Mt. Southfield a second home, but very soon during his first year I realized it was a *new* home he was making on his own, a revenge against his parents who had failed to extend his old one as far into the future as they should have, a compensation for that bungled opportunity. We had fucked up—or rather I had: the anger and bewilderment he had felt over Judith's leukemia had eventually coalesced on me as its most fulfilling target. My remarriage three years later, and Morgan's subsequent birth not long after that, further isolated him, or me from him. Whichever one of us was an island, the distance between us became a gulf; when we made tentative efforts to cross it the emotional turmoil whose ripples we confronted seemed a signal of the leviathan threatening to swallow us up.

These are my interpretive gestures, of course, an inadequate formulation through which I tried to make my ineptitude and pain accessible to myself. Martin showed a stolid courage, as I saw it, during the complex buffetings of the decade between Judith's death and another of his own life's commencements.

"So, when are we going fishing?" he'd said, dropping the question lightly as he sat down in the scorer's seat. We were honoring one of our rituals: a set at the local bowling alley, father and son together. This was in the fortunate years before the advent of the phrase "quality time." He'd just rolled a strike, his fourth in a row after an open first frame, and was in a groove.

Suddenly I had the sense there were four of us embarking on an exchange only part of which would be—or could be, now—spoken aloud. Two Martins and two Marks, on each side a visible person seconded by his own ghost playing out a silent, interior dialogue in counterpoint to the audible one.

Martin's ghost—complex, as all interior beings are—combined the dutiful son honoring the puzzling father, and the amused son humoring the silly one. He was saying something like *Well, it's time I tried to cross this awful bridge. I've met enough people at school who do things I don't understand but who I manage to accept; I should give my father the same break. But God, fishing? I don't really think I can find the meaning in that.*

"Anytime," I said. "You really interested?"

My ghost recognized—as his must have, too—the informality of this exchange, so awkward, in fact, it seemed formal. And there was my immediate, deep gratitude for this gesture, and the affection it released for my good-hearted son, coexisting with, and not contradicted by, an impatience with an idea I knew would fail so miserably I didn't want to pursue it another step.

As the thunder of falling pins reverberated around us, the ghost of the father mumbled, but clearly *I love you, but you don't have to do this; I love your desire to do this, but please, let's just let it pass.*

"Yeah. I'm curious about it," Martin said. "You've been going since I can remember—at least since Mom died. I'd like to find out firsthand what it's about."

But don't his ghost cried out *make me deal with an actual fish. Don't let me catch anything. Standing around in a cold river is all I can manage.*

"That's great," I said. "We'll go early tomorrow morning. You up to that?"

"Sure. I'm used to it from tests and stuff."

Both our ghosts cursed in unison this revolting development.

Neither of us substantial beings bowled very well after that, though Martin did manage to salvage a 180 from the game our four-voiced chorus had interrupted. Once or twice during the third game—a disaster for both of us—I wondered if this experience with its layers of silent communication was itself a replaying, an echo down time, of similar moments between my father and myself: the pulling apart and the occasion for subsequent reunion twined into one rope we held onto together.

We were up at four. Martin took from the fridge two sacks of chicken salad and pickle sandwiches Mary had made for us last night. She hadn't resisted our going as I suspected she would have—

one of her complaints was that she hadn't gotten to know Martin well before he went off to prep school, and now she saw even less of him. Accompanying that was her largely unspoken sadness that Martin and Morgan had never overcome the distance having different mothers had established between them. Morgan was a precocious eight by now, and I half expected Mary to try to convince us to take her along. She hadn't done that, either.

I took the heft of the brown bags Martin held as a sign of— well, come to think of it, I wasn't sure. Approval? Resignation? Martyrdom? Or perhaps this was a challenge, a way of saying *You want boundaries, you've got them.*

I loaded the gear in the trunk and we made the forty-minute drive to the north fork of the Shenandoah River. What traffic we saw was mostly going toward town, heading for the staggered early shifts at the mills; our side of the two-lane blacktop seemed almost a private drive. The trees—hickory, ash, sycamore, and expanses of oak—were leafing irregularly, but the first light slanting against the spring's small, new growth made a spangle of pale green and yellow above us on both sides of the road. The morning chill was still on the air, and a mist skinned the water's surface when we waded into the river.

Martin grimaced and mouthed *cold* at me. I nodded agreement, smiled. He held his rod in his left hand, his arm curved out at shoulder level as if he were hunting the fish and would pound them to death on sight.

I took his other arm and drew him farther out, to the edge of the shallows.

"This is the hard part, like I told you," I said quietly. "Getting used to the water—temperature, current, bottom. You won't have to worry much about the last one where we are—it's mostly regular. The big boulders are downstream a ways."

I repeated briefly the instructions about casting and control-ling direction that I had been through with him sometimes in the front yard when he was little. His practice tries were pretty good, considering he'd never laid a line in actual water. As far as I knew. But the Connecticut River was only a mile or so from the Mt. Southfield campus.

"Lay your lure"—we were using Rapalla minnows to minimize the chance of snags—"at either end of pools, and at the edge of the current where you can see it." As I listed a few other advices he watched the river, apparently intent on a dimpled area out from us and slightly downstream.

"A good place to start," I said. "But keep your distance. Those little whirlpools mean bigger rocks underneath, probably a ridge of them."

I pointed at a rocky spit below us about 70 yards away, where the river veered left. "Stay this side of the center until you get there"— my finger poked the air as if I could, by the extra effort, touch the clump of yellow wildflowers on the spit—"working the water across from you. Give me one of your big whistles when you get there." I dropped my arm. "I'll fish upstream."

He looked at me; in turning his shoulders he tilted his rod down so that half of it speared the water, sheared by the refraction. I lifted it against the river's gentle resistance, looking at him for an instant. The sunlight sheening the surface reflected in his eyes, flattening them, but, standing a yard from him with my hand helping lightly to support the rod he held, I caught a glimpse of how far away he already was, flowing into his life which—an apparition ghosting the geographical spot we occupied—was a river he had let me step into for a moment. The day's baptism turned out to be mine.

He waded away and began casting. I fished halfheartedly, enjoying being in the river, feeling the current press my calves, paying little attention to the Rappala wriggling across and away from me. Each time it would draw my line taut at the close of its arcing dance downstream, Martin would be in my line of sight. Eventually I left the minnow shimmying at the edge of the current and watched him.

The motion of his body and arms and rod created one rhythm, a fluidity that any lifelong fisherman would have envied. Yet there was an absence of involvement as well, visible in a tilt of his head, or the touch of his hand on the reel handle the second before he began to stir, or the way his waist cocked as he turned to change his position in the water. Not awkwardness, but a kind of displacement showing itself, the body's indications of a split between the ability—

even the adeptness—to do something and the desire to be doing something else.

About halfway to the spit he took four or five steps directly into the center of the current, evidently swifter than where it diffidently swirled about my legs. He raised the rod in his right arm above his head, beginning a movement that in its extended singularity erased the distinction between skill and unwillingness I had just remarked. As his arm climbed skyward, the rod a horizontal wand capping it, his body turned slowly—head first, then shoulders, then that part of the torso remaining above water—a slow torque that I imagined carrying all the way to his feet, tiptoed on the unseeable stones of the bottom. He gave himself thus to the river, to its motion, and floated downstream, only his head, a circle on the water—a planet in space—clearly discernible.

It was hypnotic, transporting. I mean both those terms literally. Martin's head—diminished somewhat in the distance, a part of the river—became the first focus I had been able to give myself to since the bowling alley the previous night, which seemed now a roughed-out background scene from another life.

His head in the river this morning—his sixteenth year, a junior in a venerable, challenging prep school—transposed into his head twelve years earlier, midway his fourth year, thirteen months or so before Judith died. Smaller, of course, but bearing the same close-cropped, dark hair, no part, slightly ovoid at the crown.

He is sitting in the front of a small canoe, on the bottom, leaning against the fanny-guard of the front seat, facing me, paddling. His head is bowed as he lifts from my tackle box a new lure for me to attach to the clip of my spinning rod.

"This?" He holds up a black-and-white spoon, his head still bowed.

"No. The red-and-white one. In the next tray hole."

He brings his arm down, his oversize T-shirt sleeve flapping nearly to his elbow.

"I see it." This time his head and his arm rise together. "Ready?" he asks. Serious attention. Lips folded in against his teeth.

"Yep," I say, holding my right hand out toward him. "Any time."

He tosses the spoon at the count of three. It hits the side of the canoe, just short of my hand. I fetch it in off the carom.

"Got it," I tell him.

"Yay-yah," he says, flashing me a grin. "What does that little feller do?"

Little feller is our generic term for all lures.

"It wiggles."

"They all wiggle."

I conceded that, impressed. "But some of them wiggle different from others. This one does a sideways wiggle, and look"—I pointed at the wavy red-and-white stripes—"these make it even wigglier."

"Can the fish see that?"

"Sure." I lifted the stringer out of the water and nodded at the three pickerel on it. "These guys did."

"I mean the colors and different wiggles, like that."

"Probably," I said. "But nobody knows for sure." I let the fish slip back down, the chain rattling dully against the aluminum of the canoe. "Maybe when you learn to swim you could see how they look in the water."

I clipped the daredevil on and flipped it out into the lake about six feet past his seat. "You can see what it does from up here now."

I drew it slowly past the side of the canoe. He followed its sinewy path as if he were, indeed, conducting part of a long-range experiment in which this might be the pivotal piece of data. New discoveries in the perception of aquatic life.

It was nearly 8 A.M. We were on our way in after two hours on Lake Chorcorua, where we were spending a week in a cottage a generous friend had lent us. I hadn't known much about fishing for pickerel, and was happy about the ones I'd caught. Martin had passed through the first half hour in a foggy aftermath of sleep, but since then had been as attentive to, and inquisitive about, everything—from canoe rivets to the various grassy growths on the lake bottom—as he had about the red-and-white spoon.

Pleased as I was about the fish, his company had been the real joy of the morning. Going home now to the pancakes Judith had promised us seemed the height of desire to me. Our lives together, companionable and warm, were, in fact, more than I could have asked for.

I remembered our second summer-vacation trip together, when she had tried to learn to paint. During her classes in the afternoon at a gallery in Lenox, I would haunt the lakes and ponds of western Massachusetts, to teach myself how to fish still water. It constituted my introduction to weedless worms, which I never got used to, either jigging and bouncing them on the other end of the line, or handling them, disliking their slightly sleazy feel and the thin, chemical smell they carried from whatever they were packaged in to keep them supple. They were six to eight inches long, a passable imitation of the real thing once they were immersed.

They came in all colors, even a neonlike chartreuse, and what I heard someone call bimbo purple. I used the weedless ones—a term I also had trouble accepting, since no worm I'd ever seen, plastic or otherwise, had weeds. I learned the adjective meant almost its opposite, since the hooks had thin, flexible metal filaments that acted like clips, making the hook assembly a sort of pressure-released safety pin which one could drag through weeds and grasses without tangling in them. The "hook" stayed closed under the comparatively gentle tugging of the bottom growth, but the guard would compress when a fish hit, and the barb would function normally. Weedless worms, then, were designed to be fished in weeds.

Of which there were bundles in the waters I wandered to, aimlessly for the most part, a discovery of new places, a growing list of comparative values I charted in my repertory of future choices, should we pass this way again. What was unusual—although I didn't register it then, being absorbed in the moment—was this very lack of purpose, or ambition or lust, which extended from my disinterest in where I fished, to my acceptance of bodily discomfort and the awkwardness of fishing that always accompanied it, to not feeling personally diminished if I came home with nothing on the stringer. Time disappeared as well—or consequently—or perhaps time absorbed me, became a medium I moved through with as much inattention and acceptance as I waded the lake shores.

I came home shut-out most of the time, in fact, which Judith greeted with neither chagrin nor amusement. We talked about my outings and her paintings as if they were similar explorations. My accounts were largely descriptions of locations and flora; she, in her turn, would have me run my forefinger along the grainy paper, following the trails her brush had taken. I would linger especially on little starbursts and blossoms where she had tipped the surface and the color seemed to have fled in all directions the center where it had been released, as if these points could be entrances into the painting. The paper itself rippled from the water it had absorbed.

One day I had astounding luck, bringing home three large-mouth bass, all longer than twenty-four inches and hefting close to three pounds. I cleaned them, left the smallest on the drainboard, and placed the next on a platter on the middle shelf of the fridge so that when Judith removed it she would reveal the largest on its platter a shelf beneath. She would have to remove it to get at certain essentials I had put inconveniently behind it.

That little drama played as I had imagined it might, full of surprise and excitement, but what touched us most was the way we seemed instinctively to spread this unusual intensity outward from itself, extending it into the rest of the week. The ripples widening their circumference pleased us as much as the initial experiences that had set them in motion.

Sitting in the canoe with Martin now, I realized—not a cerebral recognition, but a more integral one, as if I looked at that earlier summer set before me in one of Judith's watercolors—it was the combination of intense periods of intricately shared pleasures with relaxed extensions of contentment during which we seemed to float with our lives, buoyed, that had made the time feel whole, rhythmic, sufficient. I lingered now with our son in the memory and presence of such containment and wonder.

I paddled about thirty yards in the long, narrowing inlet toward our dock, and then turned the canoe slowly 180 degrees.

"You're going backwards."

"Yep. I want to fish a few more times where we've been."

"Say good-bye?"

"Say good-bye."

I kept the casts under the overgrowth that curved increasingly from each bank toward a central meeting above us, eventually forming an arch. The early sunlight flecked the midsummer leaves, scintillant in the intermittent breeze. I caught nothing, and had banged the canoe three or four times trying awkwardly to maintain reverse.

What turned out to be, unintentionally, my last cast began when I couldn't resist the urge to aim one directly down the midline of those impending trees. I knew better, but knowing better when you're ekeing a few last hopes out of the close of a fishing trip is as good as knowing nothing. And what I wanted to do *was* possible, though thinking that is another danger signal: the odds are against it.

Whatever slim chance I had of snaking the daredevil through that thin crevice of blue––not as straight as it looked at first, before I raised my arm—disappeared when I let the line off my finger too soon. I cast a major-league infield fly, about ten degrees off the vertical, carried higher by this lure, because of its weight, than by any other bait in the box. It zinged, too, though there's no physical explanation for such a sound; it was as if I'd launched a missile and the initial thrust left its signature in the parted air.

Minutely parted, to be sure. And for an instant of the upward arc I thought I would luck out, though the lure, when it fell, would be only an embarrassing ten feet or so beyond Martin's end of the canoe.

The breeze, however, catches the line, bellying it sideways, and the red-and-white stripes begin to turn slowly, suspended on a twig high above our heads.

Martin, who has been watching the water in front of him, turns back toward me.

"Where is he?"

I wiggle my rod, still pointing at the strip of sky. "Way up there," I say, and give the line a little tug. There is still a chance I can gentle the lure off the twig; it quivers slightly in response to my pressure.

"I see it," Martin says. "Can you get it back?"

"I'm going to try." But the angle is terrible, and if I move the canoe to improve it I'll create slack, and the breeze will add tangled line to the twigs. Pretty soon I have to revert to brute force, and it becomes clear I'll have to snip off the line.

Which I do.

A twangy *sproing* sounds, a comic echo of that outgoing *zing* some moments ago. The curly monofilament lands between us in the canoe, some of it coiling over the side and into the water.

We look at each other.

"You lost your little feller."

I turn the canoe around again.

He and I look up at the daredevil, rotating slowly among the twigs and sunkissed leaves—a bright, new growth that will bear its brilliantly lacquered surface into the fall, and then, in the bare winter when the lake freezes and people walk on water, it will be one angel of color in an otherwise appalling spread of unrelieved whiteness.

I wondered, as I reentered the Shenandoah River these twelve years apart, if that lure might still be there, not knowing how fast plastic line deteriorates when it's exposed to all weathers.

Martin had reached the rocky spit; his head appeared to be tilted back, his face absorbing the sunlight, and I thought he must be sitting on a boulder. I couldn't be sure, because the clump of yellow wildflowers obscured his body.

I began to reel in, thinking to wade down and join him. Maybe we'd eat those sandwiches for breakfast. That prospect vanished, however, when the rock I thought my Rapalla had hung on suddenly lit out for the center of the river.

It was big, whatever it was. When I recovered from my surprise I calmed down and commenced the fight. It was alternately lethargic and abrupt, not a pattern I was familiar with. *Not a carp* I thought. *Please.* I'd just as well cut the line now, as go round and round with a prehistoric hulk that looked and tasted like mud. They grew as big as eight to ten pounds in this river. There was no telling, too, how long he'd been munching my lure. It could be, by now, lodged in his gut. Odds were I wouldn't lose him.

I worked him—it was in no way playing—for maybe five minutes, being pulled gradually toward the deeper water despite my effort to get the fish to drift to the nearer bank. Finally, in a fit of disgust, I took three or four steps further out and, holding the rod up, sat down and felt the current take me.

About that time I saw Martin stand up, his movement communicating first alarm, and then puzzlement.

I waved at him with the rod, a maneuver made easy by the slack in the line my downstream journey created.

He relaxed and waved back, moving to the end of the spit, waiting in the shallows.

With only a few strokes of my free hand—at the right second, as I planned it—I would pull free of this current, regain the bottom and walk over to the spit.

If the bloody fish who had engorged my unattended lure was still on the line we would, between us, outlast him and then decide how to deal with whatever monstrosity he turned out to be.

But as I floated, borne by the current, occasionally pushing off from a rock that presented itself—strangely disengaged from everything but the water that would carry me as long as I let it, neither cold nor warm now but simply the place I happened to be—catching glimpses of my son—waterlogged himself, a rangy presence among the wildflowers and river-smoothed stones, waiting where the river had taken him—I thought better of it.

I brought my arm down so the rod lay reel up just in the river's topmost membrane, feeling the beginning tugs against its length. And I let it go, too.

In the first year of our marriage, my wife Callie and I spent two or three days at a rustic retreat in the Massanutten Mountains. It was in the long waned days of my fishing, well into choice. We walked to the pond the slick, fold-out brochure described as "isolated yet fetching," and found its shores a tangle of vines—honeysuckle and wild grape and rose— nearly inaccessible except for a six-foot space where the jungle thinned sufficiently for a determined fisherman to force a small johnboat through into the algae-ridden water.

Though I had no gear with me I felt a little of the old pull. The fading relationship incompletely transmuted. As if a voice, or the echo of its diminution, played a light ripple of regret and I tilted my head toward it.

What's this music creeping by me on the waters?

Though no observer would have seen our visit as other than ordinary and predictable, it was in such delicately meshed interior devotions altogether remarkable.

We talked of our grandparents and their acceptance of us, wholly unintentional in their saving ways, giving an opening to each of us for the continuing pattern of return and replenishment as our futures thickened and overwhelmed. We laughed at the degree of ancestor worship we both inadvertently practiced, soft-pedaling the genuflection, crying at the image of ourselves, our hands clasped together before us in the attitude of greeting, or prayer, or parting, bowing toward no shrine but the pardoning memory of the figures we had internalized, enmeshed wholly in the center of ourselves.

Our lovemaking took part of its gentle ferocity from these presences, honoring our multiple shadows, aware that the indelible impressions of less comforting preemptive kin were involved as well, and that those forces led into other, less reparable frays.

Oh heart, oh troubled heart, another poet says, and though we were still comparatively young, I remember his calling, remembered in our passion that mountain jack-rabbit's impression on the bent grass after the creature itself had vanished.

What we brought back with us, though—what became the chord by which we evoked that quiet, settling retreat—were the fireflies.

We had gone once again, at late dusk, to the pond. On our return we stopped on a rise and looked back at the water's darker expanse. Beside it, covering the meadow—not as far as the eye could see, which in any case would not have been very far given the encroaching night and the low wattage of their illuminations—and sharply limited by its cedar-hemmed borders, were immoderate fireflies, carrying on their bipolar flashing. Thousands of them, or so it seemed.

Their flight was itself invisible, an inference from the incessant shifting of the locations of their individual lights. Among the sudden implausibilities—although we "knew," as we are in the habit of saying, what the mechanics of the insect experience were—was the impression that no glow lit the same spot twice. As unusual as the nonrepetitiveness of snowflakes, in a situation where repetition and predictability were otherwise the norm.

In spite of the vivacity of the lights, all was still, or all else was still. We watched, stilled ourselves. Callie told me later she had held her breath as if she had been under water (a pond of light, I thought, as she spoke), until, at full dark, the display gradually faded, going nowhere. A long time to hold your breath I said, and she said, yes.

In the aftermath, as we stood among the surround of crickets, their sound replacing in the scheme of things the visual panoply the fireflies had given us, she said,

"Yvette would have loved that."

"She would have," I said. "It's too bad you can't invite people you love to see things they'd especially care for."

"No, it's not," Callie said.

I smiled in the dark. "You're right," I said. I touched her shoulder. "But we can ask her to visit, and take her somewhere where special things are possible."

"Where's that?" she asked.

"Anywhere," I said, before I thought.

It isn't a dream, but parts of the drive toward Cobbs Creek, and other, scattered aspects of the whole day—intrusions of light, inflections from the periphery—seemed like it could have been. The road down, for instance: arrow straight, a diminishing convergence of grays—the tree line, the wide shoulders, the pavement—all centered on the white line aimed through their heart, toward a heart. A painting Edward Hopper might have dreamed of. We moved on it in the predawn as if the car were mist coagulated just enough to support us, silently drawn—in both senses: pulled along by some force emanating from ourselves but seeming as well to be out there, a magnet at the river; and sketched by some hand into the picture we drove through, were part of—drawn overland like a hovercraft.

When the sun rose and cut through this dreamscape, it was sudden. The monochrome wasn't broken, but replaced, gray transposing into an unspecified brightness that surrounded us. The car became solid again, a bone-crushing heaviness plunging through the early morning as if to release itself from gravity.

And as suddenly we were just two people in a Buick wagon driving Route 198 to spend a day fishing on the Piankatank.

"Nice morning," my father says.

I murmur agreement, shift in the seat, move my hands to the top of the steering wheel.

"I like the way the sun finally clears off the mist." He rolls his window down about four inches. The air has begun to warm. His pudgy hands fidget about on his lap, pulling at his trousers, then the seat cover. It's hard to imagine him tossing off set shots in college, leading the old Southern Conference in assists. He rests his left palm on the seat and curls the fingers of his right hand into the cleft of the armrest on the door. He pushes a little against the pillow behind his back.

"You need to stop and walk around?" I ask.

"Naw. It's only twelve miles. I'll walk some while you and Mike get the boat ready."

"Mike'll have the boat ready."

"Yeah. Well, it'll keep while I get the kinks out." He looks over and smiles. "Before I spend the day getting them back in."

He wants me to say, "We don't have to do this," but he doesn't know it, is unaware at sixty-nine of his most precious rituals, the little shapes his needs push into the world, transient, repetitive. I don't say anything. In the elongated instant—a bubble of time—in which I choose to be silent, don't take his bait, another dreamlike suspension occurs, a superimposition on our current unfulfilled exchange of a moment fifteen years ago when, very much against his continuous assertions of unwillingness, my first wife and I had "carried" him two hundred miles round-trip into a gorge for a picnic.

It had been a perfect April day. The sun vibrated on the new leaves—sycamores, oaks, and maples mostly—which the breeze ruffled; the river was high with snowmelt, breaking into sparkles and rapids where it usually practiced lazy evasions of the smooth boulders that studded the stretch where we had settled. We ate, we walked, we separated and mused. It could have been an idyll peopled by untroubled miniatures, but underneath every word we spoke or gesture we made was my father's grousy dissatisfaction, his disgruntlement at having his Saturday of football and bourbon destroyed.

But when we got back, and, in the weeks following, he spoke of our outing to acquaintances, it was as if he'd planned everything, as if his heart had found the holy place of its beginnings. He'd never had a better time. He'd forgotten how beautiful the outdoors could be. One ought to spend more time with one's children; after all, we weren't getting any younger.

We still aren't, of course—have deepened the worn ruts of ourselves, becoming what we are, far too long to turn back; but I have also burrowed deeply enough into my hidden networks to find a compromise. "We don't have to stay out all day," I say. "You know how monotonous it is when nothing's biting. We'll get a slack tide after noon. We could quit then."

"We'll see." He adjusts the pillows again. His left hand comes up to his nose and under the guise of scratching it with his forefinger he digs inside with his thumbnail.

We crunch up to Mike's restaurant and marina on a new apron of gravel. The sunlight on the mica flecks in the crushed stone creates a spread of dazzle around us. Until we pull into the shade of the building I feel as if we're driving on another element, neither earth nor water, but the two merged with light. The tires spit stones against the undercarriage, seem to be fighting a tendency to sink. My father and I rock briefly with the sway.

When I turn off the engine, the sudden quiet—a beaching, a relief —lasts maybe ten seconds, and Mike is upon us, opening doors, prying apart the jaws of the tailgate and its window, having our rods leaning beside the restaurant entrance before we're through stretching.

Mike is about six feet tall, and bulky. As he and Seth shake hands, I am shocked once again how small my father seems beside most other men. My childhood perception of him as a giant I had to lift my eyes skyward to see remains the unconscious perspective I carry with me, no matter how often I have it corrected. The solid man exchanging greetings with his old friend is briefly surrounded by the shadow of my earliest image of him, as if compacted from it.

I'm five-ten or so myself, not far from forty, and even as I realize I still imagine my father to be taller than I am, Mike greets me with a version of How big you've gotten he tries ineptly to adapt to current circumstances.

I tell him only my fingernails and nose are still growing. "But I've got a son who'd really surprise you."

"I'm sorry," Mike says. "I don't see you guys very often. You know how it is." He lays his arm across Seth's shoulders and steers him toward the restaurant. "I forget it's not twenty years ago at Russell's, and we're all young peckers again, rarin' to go."

I follow them inside, noticing how my father's body seems infinitesimally to lean into Mike's for support.

The last year or so he has gone stretches of two, sometimes three, weeks without needing the oxygen system that was set up in his bedroom four years ago. The two slim, green tanks stand in the corner like grotesquely elongated udders, their nipple ends joined by a tube which then drops to the breathing apparatus by his chair. It's green, too—a hollow rectangular cube about a foot square and eight inches high, with interior medicinal compartments connected by valves the pressure of the patient's breathing operates—but because of the transparent plastic of which it's made it takes on in any light an eerie, angulated radiance, so the elements of the system seem almost comically mismatched: on the one hand the tubes of oxygen, scarred and scratched as if they were relics raised countless fathoms from the ocean's bed, and, on the other, the breathbox, sleek and luminous, designed for a voyage to outer space.

Though his dependency on this system has decreased in the past months, and though he had a session with it last night, he sits down at the first table he comes to, and places his hands on his knees so his elbows jut outward, the posture he always uses when he has trouble breathing. He takes a couple of deep inhalations—deep, that is, for him, the continuing flexibility of whose lungs is now a medical mystery. He looks sideways at me and shakes his head barely. "It's OK," he mouths.

It's OK.

I wonder if we should have tried this.

I wonder who talked who into it, at what point our separate, frayed desires twined closely enough to take on the anonymous, exterior momentum we have ridden this far.

Magic carpet.

It's not too late to articulate the fear thinning the already thin air under us, but neither of us says it: what do we—I—do if he needs oxygen while we're in the boat?

Mike is too busy at the grill to notice our brief, private niche in his flurry. We eat the eggs and bacon he fries, spread butter and opulent marmalade on the toast which pops partway into the air from an old-fashioned toaster, nearly ejected as in a cartoon, and then falls with a rattle back into its slots.

Our table overlooks the marina. Two weeks ago, around Labor Day, the whole place would have been a warren of people putting their boats to sleep for the winter. Today Mike seems the final stray, all that communal energy and motion finding its last wags in his isolated fussing with this and that—arranging his staple items in locked cabinets, hosing out his walk-in freezer, outfitting and feeding off-season stragglers like us.

The glare on the picture windows deepens their plane against the air of the restaurant, making the place seem walled, cavernous. We could have been abandoned here, for the feel of it, our voices small and incipient with echoes, the dust motes already lazily swimming down the shafts of sunlight.

"How you feeling?" Mike straddles a chair he's turned backwards to our table, sipping occasionally from a double-size cup of black coffee. It's the same coffee I'm drinking but it moves in his cup like sludge. "You really up to this after all you been through?"

"Hell, Mike, that was three, four years ago. Ancient history." Seth wipes toast crumbs from his mouth with a paper napkin, preoccupied with the gesture as an actor stresses a bit of minor stage business he can control to divert attention from more complex matters he's less sure of. He watches his hands spread the napkin in his lap, smoothing it against his old, gray pants. "Mark's doing all

the grunt work anyhow. I'm along for the ride." The phrase pleases
him. He looks up at me, then at Mike. "Literally. I don't have to lift
a thing except my leg into the boat."

"Hey, that's the way," Mike says. He looks around us at the rest
of the room. "Wish I had me somebody to lighten the load here.
Don't seem like much now, but it gets hairy sometimes."

His right hand starts toward the pocket of his red-and-black plaid
flannel shirt, but stops before his fingers can raise the flap. The
pocket is flat. I realize Mike has left his cigarettes somewhere so he
won't smoke while Seth's here.

"If you could use me year round," I say, "I'd quit my job tomorrow
and come down for good."

"What would your boss say?"

"I *am* my boss."

"Can't offer you any bennies, son. But the work's good."

"I know it is," I say. "And the place."

"Well, maybe. It's been good to me, I guess. But I been here so
long I can't get separate from it any more. Routine. You know."

"Yeah," I say. "It swallows you up."

"Don't it." He swings his leg up as if he's dismounting a horse.
"But that's what you guys came down here to get away from. Come
on. I'll push you off."

Seth has less trouble than I anticipated getting into the skiff.
He holds my shoulder and puts his right leg over the side. The
momentum of his left going in makes him have to turn, shuffling
his feet around to keep his balance. With his arms out he looks
sort of graceful, a novice dancer learning a part. He sits on the
center seat.

Mike has forgotten the gas feeder can so I lug it down from the
storage bin by one of the sailboat slips. The empty forest of masts
at this end of the marina is a lean anticipation of what the wooded
shoreline will look like in another month or so.

The gas can bumps my thighs as I negotiate the softer sand on this
part of the beach. It thuds against the bottom of the boat hollowly
when I set it down, losing my grip at the last instant.

"Hey, you'll scare the fish away," my father says, glad for a chance
to repeat a familiar part of the ritual.

"What fish there are," is my line, diminishing expectations, suggesting our humility to any ancient spirits of the water who might be listening.

"I put a couple extra sheer pins in the tool kit," Mike says. He fetches two cushions from the storage bin and hands them to me. "Forgot these. My mind mostly turns off when the season's over, but I think that's everything. You guys fill up the keeper, OK?"

"Sure," Seth says.

"He'll catch 'em all," I say. "You know how it is when you're in the same boat with the fish vacuum."

"Yeah. I do." He smiles at Seth, or memories of the two of them, and pushes us free of the sand, walking a foot or two into the river's edge. "Call me if you need me."

I release the outboard, its props and shaft knifing into the water, leaving a thick, twisting seam in the surface behind us. I tighten it down and yank the cord. The motor catches, its throaty rumbling smoothing out immediately, sounding well-tuned and dependable. Mike waves from the shallows, his figure already smaller, a dark shape against the sunshingled sand.

I turn to face Seth, set my hand comfortably on the tiller's rubber-handled cover—all but one of its finger guides broken off—and head for deep water.

"Trust," my father says, curling a green shrimp onto his hook. "That's what matters. You have to make the critters trust what they see. So much so they'll bite even when they're not hungry. Wouldn't even sit down at the table."

He lets his line out until the sinker hits bottom, then reels in six or eight inches and begins gently jigging his bait. To me it appears a measured routine—and, of course, it is; he renders it rhythmical as well, patterns still responsive to numbers and repetition, but to this he adds his indefinable touch, an intuition about his *prey's* rhythms, a sense of the life he intrudes upon. Bart Fenwick used to say my father had been a fish in a former life, a whale who knew exactly what waters to swim in, where smaller subjects schooled as if they wanted to be his next meal.

He is never embarrassed to speak of fishing in terms such as *trust* and *love*. I've heard him talk at least once about the sacrifice involved, the mutual giving up by fish and fisherman of their individual appetites to the larger design of predation inherent in the universe.

"Sometimes," he said, "I don't feel like it's me holding the pole. I'm not even there."

The river's surface looks as flat and impervious as a pane of glass, our skiff a hub at the center of a vast clock face with no hands. The acute angles formed by rod and line and the ovals of stacked head and torso would be, to an observer in the distance, the only deformities in this sleek geometry.

It's almost noon.

We've finished the tuna sandwiches and, in spite of my opposition—not all that intense—Seth's had a beer as well. He boats another spot and slips it in the keeper tank attached to the bottom of the boat. We have talked little for over four hours. I've told him about Yvette Wu's two little bluegill, and a short version of Joe Skins' muskie, but the rest of the time has passed marked mostly by the sound of the boat in the water, and ourselves in the boat. A group of gulls gave us a raucous salute as they passed heading upriver about an hour ago. For a while—off and on, in fact—I have worried he is enduring all this, in pain somewhere, but his breathing has been clear and regular and he shows no more than the ordinary signs of discomfort when he performs the fisherman's simple movements, baiting, casting, reeling in, adjusting his butt on the boat cushion.

"Sure is still," he says.

"Like the moon." Our voices fall flatly on the air. I think if they were coins and we threw them they would be too light to skip on the water. "We could be astronauts."

"Like the grave," he says. He points at the tree line with his rod, the sinker and unbaited hook swaying, a pendulum Dali might have painted. "If you stuck your fingers in the ground over there it'd be loamy and black. There'd be pieces of last year's leaves still decaying. It would be soft and damp." He lets the rod down slowly until it rests on the gunwale. "Full of life. If you planted something there, boy would it grow."

His enthusiasm is as soft as he imagines the ground to be, a caressing of his words in which, though I am predisposed to hear it because of the difficulties of his recent life, I don't detect even a hint of longing. He sounds like a scientist testing a hypothesis in the lab.

"I tasted dirt once."

"I expect you tasted it a lot of times," I say, "running the ball into those giants."

"Well, not counting that. I mean"—a childlike curiosity touches his words now, and he cocks his head slightly—"I ate some on purpose, off my fingertips. It was out near the fishpond section of Maud and Russell's backyard." He looks at me. His eyes are calm as the water around us, but they dazzle inward, a new star beginning its unimaginable coalescence. "You know, out by the grape arbors."

I do know. I tell him I used to spend a lot of time out there by myself, feeding the goldfish, listening to the bees fumble among the bunches of grapes. I loved to pop their purple skins and feel the pale green fruit slide past my lips like secrets I would never keep, they tasted so good.

"Without that dirt," he says, "the grapes wouldn't have been that sweet. But the dirt, that's different."

I wait for him to tell me how. I reel in and find my bait gone, a pattern of the day so far for me. I didn't feel even a nudge.

"It had no temperature. I thought it would be warm from the sun, or maybe cool like it felt to my fingers, but it just *was*, you know? I couldn't figure that out. Still can't."

"What'd it taste like?"

He hasn't rebaited his hook, hasn't moved the rod from its resting place. He's still looking at me.

"You were out there while I was working?"

"Yes. A lot. There and under the big elms in the front yard. I even walked out on the dock sometimes, and lay down to watch the water through the spaces in the boards."

"Funny. I always thought of you with Maud or Russell, or one of the maids."

"Sometimes I was, when it suited." I don't feel like going into that old phrase, that shuffling among whoever wasn't overwhelmed with one chore or another.

"I'd go out there, too. Late at night. Watch the stars through the grapevines." He turns his head away from me and tilts his rod slowly upwards, not so much following as looking at the invisible arc its tip traces against the sky. "All tangled up." He twirls the tip slightly, like a fencer warming up. "But it was daytime when I tasted the dirt. About this time of day. About lunchtime."

He lays the rod on his lap, gently, as if it were as brittle as a strand of thin spaghetti. He stares at it, runs his thumb and forefinger along a section between line guides—back and forth, back and forth, absently. He stops. His hand relaxes on his knee.

"I had a picture of your grandfather I used to carry in my wallet. Only picture in there besides one of you and Luke and your mother. You remember it?"

"I don't know." I had my own favorite snapshot of Russell I kept on my desk. "What'd it look like?"

"He was standing at the stern of the canoe—you know, that thirty-foot boat he was working in when you fell off the dock—standing up there holding the tiller in one hand. Casual as all hell, facing forward—whoever took the picture must have been standing close to the wheel. His body"—my father shifted on the seat cushion— "was so relaxed, that impressed me, loose *under* his clothes like those ratty white pants and shirt were on top of it. He held that tiller with his fingertips, easy, like"—he paused, searching for the simile he wanted—"like you might hold a pen you weren't writing with."

He looked down at the handle of the rod lying across his knees. "You know what I mean?"

He seemed not to expect me to say anything, so I didn't.

"Like he knew what the thing was for and was ready to use it when it suited him. When he had to." He ran his forefinger lightly over the knob at the end of the rod. He tilted his head to the side and looked at me. I thought I saw tears in his eyes.

"But his face, that was what—he had on one of those old dressy hats he used to wear, all beat up and out of shape, but still snazzy. It cast a shadow that hid his eyes. You couldn't really see them. But from the rest of his face—rimmed, I remember, by light on each cheek and at one side of his chin—you could tell what was in his eyes. What expression."

He stopped and looked past me over the water. His body tightened. He wanted to stand up. He didn't. He couldn't. He gripped his rod in both hands, raised it about four inches and brought it down hard against his thighs. Only when he sighed and relaxed and spoke again did I realize he'd been gritting his teeth.

"His face was tired. Whatever he knew. Tired, but determined not to be."

He bowed his head and I thought he was finished, but after a minute—a long silence on the still river—he spoke softly again. "It wasn't a hard expression—he got that when he got mad. But it made a hardness in the picture, like what was in his head had gotten stuck there; the rest of his body in that picture hadn't been informed."

"Or the rest of the world?" I asked. "Like Maud? Like us?"

He considered. "Yes, I reckon that, too," he said. "Since he died I've felt sometimes there were things he could have told me. But he never did."

How many sons—or sons-in-law—have sung that refrain I wonder now, and may have then, but I said nothing. I didn't ask him what he would have wanted my grandfather to tell him or again what that dirt tasted like. Some questions, especially at the moment perfectly molded for their asking, are their own obstacle, opportunities thwarted by themselves. And if he had known, he wouldn't have been torn by the terrible nostalgia that photograph focused for him. It would have become just another item of affection in the album.

I want a camera now, myself, for this moment, a black-and-white suspension, almost a silhouette, of my father's finding words—brief, unsettled—and making shapes with them that take no more palpable a place in time than the motion of his rod tip through the air. I want to record his body against the light, with a hint at its edges of an implausible absorption, or merging of the two, that is in the negative and has not been, by some fine artistic manipulation, achieved in the darkroom.

As if by prior agreement, we move at once, he to rerig his rod for trolling, I to start the motor for the voyage back to Mike's marina.

We cruise along until I can see the buoy marking the inlet whose end the marina nestles into, a mile or so off the port bow. The Evinrude has run like a top all day, without a miss or tick, but for reasons known only to those ancient spirits we must have insufficiently placated, it suddenly sputters, shaking wildly on its mount, and dies.

No amount of yanking and cursing and cajoling gets it going again. I try all the tricks my father can think of, but none of them works. The fuel line is open. The feeder can is half full. There's no flooding, hardly a whiff of gas from the motor. Carburetor's clean. And so on. Even the old joke about holding your mouth right fails to work, or, indeed, evoke more than a weak drain of laughter from each of us.

"I'll have to row in," I say. "You come on back here first."

Before we can change seats, however, I notice the second stage in our little drama. I wonder if this is the beginning of a run of such minor disasters, Fate's way of drawing up the stillness of the morning into a series of explosions, a kind of punctuation inserted into the subtler modulations of our own desultory dialogues. There are no oars in the boat.

"Mike can't think of everything," Seth says.

"Yes he can," I say. "He bloody well can. He thought of the sheer pins. We're going fishing in eight fathoms of river, with no structure, and he remembers the bloody sheer pins."

We sit there a moment, wrought up in our sympathy for and condemnation of Mike, the absent focus of our disbelief. It's more practical than being angry at those spirits only because we can confront Mike with the experience. Eventually.

I've gotten to the point where I can no longer escape the seriousness of our situation through levity or anger when I see it. I point to the bottom of the boat between Seth and the bow.

"He remembered the plank," I say. "Reach down behind you and pick up the end of the thing and slide it to me. No, to your right. Yeah. Feel it?"

He turns his whole body as if his cushion were a lazy Susan, until his knees bump the seat. "I feel it. I think." He puts one foot up on the seat, his knee almost in his face, and tilts himself toward the end of the plank. I fear for an instant he will topple over, like the outsized man on the tricycle in cartoons, but just as I begin to rise and reach to help him he rights himself, holding the end of the plank.

He hefts it to get a better grip, lowers his leg, and slides over his seat what will be our makeshift means to shore: an old board, about five-and-a-half feet long, that looks like it's been ineptly ripped from a one-by-six piece of walnut. A classy substitute for an oar, anyhow, even if it's wider at one end than the other, and ragged along the edge where someone tore it from the original piece of lumber. It's also waterlogged. No telling how long it's lain in the boat—long enough, at least, for Mike to take it for part of the bottom and not see it.

"Ouch," my father says as I drag the plank from his hand.

"Sorry," I say. "Bad?" I prop the plank against my knee.

He looks at the pads on the rim of his palm. "Naw." He pulls two or three splinters from his hand and sucks the small bosses of blood away, looking up at me once, his gray eyes blank. He doesn't spit. His hand settles on his knee—palm up, fingers slightly curled—as though it's a casualty at rest. Blood begins to bubble minutely at one wound. He wraps a handkerchief around his hand and grips it lightly, as if it were a handle to something.

Our trip back to Mike's is a comedy of increasingly impossible alternatives, all focused on how I can best hold the plank for paddling. Where to sit is a relatively simple matter. I have two choices, port and starboard—after the better part of an hour I've scuttled the marine lingo for *left* and *right*, which, by then, is how I'd like to tackle the whole fiasco; I can hear Don Dunphy calling the blow-by-blow: "Another left and *another* right. I've never seen anything like it. Random is crucifying the Piankatank River. And yet he can't put it away. What resilience, what absorption! Other fighters will be copying the Piankatank's training routine after this one, you can bet on that. That river can take a punch!"

So I move back and forth from one side to the other, the skiff tilting with my weight, the one advantage I eke out of the situation. I am at least closer to the water on the side I paddle from, which gives me better leverage.

But the plank. Ah, the plank. I develop a relationship to it similar—in its unavoidable intimacy, in my ambivalent emotional tangle with it—to my relationship with my brother Luke. I hate it, I want to throw it into the water as Polyphemus hurled stones at arrogant Ulysses, I can't do without it, I would be trapped toward darkness in this little tub—my father's muscles stiffening, his breathing becoming shallower—I caress it, I want to choke it, I drag it through the water, I ease it through the water.

I try both ends with equal ineffectiveness, and equal discomfort, small rows of striations gradually developing on my fingers and palms where the sawn ends of the plank rub them. After a while the skin begins to split; after a while I quit picking the splinters the ripped side of the board has an inexhaustible supply of.

But we move. The skiff edges closer to the buoy. Or seems to, if I glance up to measure our progress infrequently enough, a discipline in itself.

I'm grateful the wind doesn't rise.

Seth is quiet again for a bit. He offers to take a turn, and would, but I refuse to allow it. In the midst of my embroilment with the board I can sense his frustration and helplessness.

"It's OK, Daddy," I tell him once, inadvertently slipping into my old way of addressing him. It seems, somehow, appropriate, as if its reminder evens up the dependencies. "It's not as wretched as it must look": my lie becomes just another unremarkable stitch in the fabric of the afternoon.

We are about halfway in when he says, "I want to apologize to you."

His tone—committed but hesitant, as if his voice is withdrawing from itself, a thinner sound than I have ever heard come from his mouth—lets me know his apology has nothing to do with the circumstances we find ourselves in at the moment.

I don't say anything. The board scrapes the side of the skiff. We make our small, incremental advance on the river's flat radiance.

"Your divorce—. When you came home to tell your mother and me about your divorce. That night."

I glance at him. He's sitting erect on the cushion, adjusting himself. He's spooled in his plug; his rod angles toward me, its reel out of sight in front of his seat.

I paddle.

"I mean after you told us. Later. You were downstairs—no, you were coming up the stairs. You seemed so far away down there. The whiskey did that, I guess. Mostly."

He stops. He nests his hands in his lap.

I look at the board, at the intricate grain of the tree flattened between my fingers, its curving expenditure, its pressed pattern repeating downward until the water refracts it, bends it illogically into another plane.

"I, uh, told you I thought I had raised *two* good sons."

I have been able to live with that sentence—ingrained in my mind—because I have always thought he was too drunk at that moment to have heard himself, much less remember, standing at the bannister railing above me, leaning on the hand gripping it, balancing, his face flushed through the rich stubble, his mouth drawn down at the corners by drink, or his distorted effort to create an impression that would disguise his condition but which only more grotesquely betrayed it, his body elongated by my inferior perspective, the judgment falling as a physical object, a slab of infinite thickness, words being only the filaments it was suspended from that enabled him to lower it upon me.

Such insubstantial sounds.

Such terrific weight.

I move the plank through the molasses we are mired in.

"I, uh, you know that fish you lost for—who was it?"

"Joe Skins."

"Yea, him. That muskie. You shouldn't be so hard on yourself about that. You did the best you could with the stuff you had in the boat."

His tone suggests a recovery, a coming forward out of the over-rehearsed aridity in which his speech had begun.

I look up at him. He has relaxed from the rigidly upright posture, a boy let loose from the hampering desk of the schoolroom, with its round, staring hole for the obsolete inkwell. He has been looking at me.

Our eyes meet. I let the board trail in the water.

"He's forgiven you for that fish a long time ago."

He doesn't say *forgive yourself*. It would involve too complex a displacement for him, plunge him into a depth from which no crane would ever hoist him, and I am grateful to him for stopping at his best edge. I can meet him there.

"You're probably right," I say, digging the poor excuse for an oar into the miraculous water that supports us, over which we make our way.

I get out of the dinghy about fifty feet from the cap of the inlet, and pull it the rest of the way by the tow rope. I drag its snubbed keel into the sand, giving it a final jerk to be sure it's firmly entrenched.

"I'll get Mike to help," I tell Seth.

The restaurant is empty, however, and locked. I'm about to start back down to the sand when I see a piece of folded paper stuck to the door glass with masking tape. *Randoms* is scrawled on it, the *s* partly obliterated by the tape.

The note says, "Had to go to town—water main busted. Hope you didn't need the oar! M."

Fuck him I think, but I'm already smiling at the kick Daddy will get out of this little touch that's a veneer to me, but which he will recognize reflexively as central to the life he shares with his old friends.

When I get back to the skiff he is still sitting on the cushion, as if he expects the boat to continue its voyage, somehow adapted so it can move next up the beach, handling the sand as if it were more water. He hasn't budged except to turn half around so he's looking back, his eyes following the line of trees along the shore of the inlet toward the main body of the river.

I'm not sure he hears me return.

I stand at the prow of the skiff a moment. He says something, half whisper, half mumble—"Let's go home," I think. In profile his face appears relaxed, receptive, his lips parted, but there is a slight tension in his body, as if he's imparting a wish to the boat whose center seat the fingertips of his spread hands just touch, almost quivering, not able to press down against the worn, deepening wood, or to give it up.

Bright Wings

WHAT MATTERED was where she put her foot. She knew that. She knew that one foot and then another planted on the ground made up her going, amounted to the Lord's way for her, or her way on the Lord's earth, which was the same thing.

The Bible said *They who have ears to hear, let them hear* and *They who have eyes to see, let them see.* It should have said *They who have feet to walk, let them walk,* too. She meant to limit that injunction just to the walking, with no morality added. There were enough references in that fat book to walking upright in the eyes of the Lord, and walking the way one *should* go. What she missed was an understanding of the walking itself, how important that was without any judgment about how you did it and who was watching larded on to it.

A body making her way, that was enough.

Praise that.

Sufficient unto the day is the walking therein.

Her feet this morning followed one another deliberately up the three rubber-padded steps of the number-six bus. She kept her eyes on first the left—a string from the big toe of her white cotton sock poked out an inch between the closely netted straps of a brown sandal—and then the right—not a whole sandal here because she had cut part of it away to give the bunion next to the ball room to take the air, a little promenade of its own. The rear of each sandal flapped in the air as she picked her feet up, and rejoined her flattened heel as she placed it on the grooved rubber above.

One at a time now.

Been doing this since they invented the bus.

Hauling this body up these triangles. Seem too small to need much lifting. But these is deep steps, yes they is. I'd as leave be climbing up a well.

When she finished the little curve the stepwell made up into the bus's main aisle, she stopped, one foot set beside the other, symmetrical except for the semi-independent bunion. She hugged her left elbow to herself and pushed down against her waist with it, appearing to adjust her dress, as if that side tended to ride up when she climbed stairs, but she was really checking to see that the folded bills for Woolworth's were still safely tucked into the wide band of her underwear. She moved her shoulders—a tiny shrug—to the right as if to realign herself, and snipped open the little change purse she had been holding before her in both hands during the thirty minutes she had waited at the bus stop.

It took two tries because at first her fingers slipped on the clasp and she had to rub them on her dress to dry them. Then the two little metal snail horns released their pressure on each other, enabling her to hook a forefinger into the purse's dark mouth. She snagged her nail on a laddered section of the lining and had to disengage it without pulling it out, drawing the lining with it and spilling her change. It never rolled far because of the grooves in the floor pad, and some kind person usually had picked it up before she could maneuver into the stooping necessary to reach it.

My body so close to the ground, funny it take so long to get down there for a dime. But here, I got it. No bending over today. No *Thank you, sir.*

She had poked into the space between the lining and the coarse outside fabric of the purse and found the familiar dime and nickel. Balancing them on the tip of her finger, she eased them into contact with her thumb, and in that curled grip—thumb on the buffalo, forefinger on FDR, a miniature crane moving slowly across the dusty air between her and the driver—she carried her money from purse to fare box and dropped it in.

It tumbled down the miniature stairwell, jingling.

The driver flicked a lever on his side of the box, two flaps yawned, and her coins disappeared.

Time that boy ran off with it, though. Acted like he was helping. Watching me out the corner of his eye all the time. Arm reaching into the bus to get my coin, body already edging back out.

Gone before I could yell. Before I could yell I was chuckling anyhow. He must've needed that money more'n me.

She turned in that jingling memory to face down the aisle. She began walking toward the rear of the bus. One face back there, but I don't recognize it. Still got my eyesight. She watched her feet shuffle over the wide white line that marked the end of the grooved surface and the beginning of the dull green smoothness of the bus's main floor. She stepped carefully on the white lettering stenciled next to the line, upside down to her now: *Passengers must stand behind white line.*

Way behind:

a reflex which no smile or chuckle accompanied.

The bus made two more stops before she negotiated the scarred aisle and reached the bench stretching across its rear end. She nodded to the stranger sitting next to the curbside window but he was absorbed in watching the abandoned storefronts at the edge of town, the skinned dirt and the candy wrappers and cigarette butts that littered it, the upheaved, broken sidewalks, the gray glass.

Queen Street, hunh? Some queen.

Then she noticed the man was asleep. All this stopping and lurching and he's asleep. Wonders.

She managed before the bus started off again to execute a 180-degree turn a few degrees at a time, her heels establishing a kind of movable pivot on which the length of her feet inscribed their slow arc, until she was able to raise herself on her toes, give a push off and plop down on the seat.

Never cease.

The momentum given her by the bus's sudden jerk forward firmly ensconced her against the ungiving back of the seat, her small fanny comfortably wedged in the 90-degree angle it made with the thinly padded bench. Her sandals hung six inches or so above the floor, their loose heels letting them release a little. She felt the air touch her through the thin socks.

Rest, feet. More coming.

She meant more walking once she got to the Woolworth's corner at the new end of Queen Street, but the phrase threw her—giving herself to the sway of the bus, relaxing—back into the kitchen of the big house where she worked.

"There'll be more people coming for dessert, Delia," Mrs. Marshall had told her three days before the dinner party, early enough for her to plan two additional Lady Baltimores and get Mr. Teichnor's delivery boy to bring in some extra sherbet. Just the same, it had seemed an undue burden had been unloaded on her, and when Mrs. Marshall had left the kitchen, afternoon bottle of sherry in hand, Delia had rested her fingers on the edge of the cutting table and stared at her feet.

She felt as if her weight had doubled and was aimed like a plummeting stone straight down her body into them; she knew they were too frail to endure such a crash, their birdlike metatarsals and brittle arches being designed just for the body they normally carried over the ground. So she redirected the fall whose potential conclusion was frightening her irrationally: she stopped gazing at her feet, encased in the secondhand white nurse's shoes she had that morning freshly coated with polish, marveling as usual at the little brush attached by a thin shaft to the cap of the bottle. Who thought that up? Man sitting in a room. Nothin to do but make up things like that.

She made herself look across the green linoleum, one patch of little raised rectangles at a time, taking her mind slowly away from the extra chores just laid upon her, feeling her looking across the expanse of floor as if she walked out of herself, left behind these feet, released them from all the pressures that bore them ever toward the earth.

Like a desert. Ridin a camel. Sunshine.

She raised her eyes when she reached the edge of the stove, let their gaze ease up the twin oven doors, past the black gouge the size of a quarter in the porcelain next to the handle of the right one, and rest finally in the sunlight pooled on the yellow wall behind it. She felt lighter again, herself.

Seen the glory. Right here in the kitchen. Not even mine. Went all that way and never took a step.

She drummed her fingers on the table, humming randomly phrases from "The Battle Hymn of the Republic."

Nothin but a cake or two. One more call to the grocery. Ain't no big thing. What I be doin acting like this?

Sitting on the bus, one hand beside her against the seat to keep from being pitched forward at the frequent stops, she still hadn't figured out why she had felt so suddenly weighted with herself that day. Or why the same thing had happened twice more since, once as she climbed the plank steps of her front porch, and again while she was at her own kitchen window, watching the sparrows peck dust under the mimosa. She had brought herself out of the heaviness by repeating what she had done the first time, moving her gaze slowly away and finally upward—following the wood grain of the last porch step, its floor, past the sag and up a supporting four-by-four to a corner of sky; the other time a sparrow's jerky path to the base of the hedge, then into it, then airborne toward her neighbor's eaves.

It had been following the hopping and the flight of those birds that had moved her present purpose. Lines from one of her favorite hymns had come lilting into her mind —

> His eye is on the sparrow
> And I know he watches me.

Why don't I get me a sparrow? *My* eye can be on it, too. And His eye be closer to me. Don't have to be a real one, can be a wooden one, can be a model.

Thus she conceived her pilgrimage to the bounty stocked under Woolworth's gold and red banner.

Each time she had felt herself take the journey of her looking, felt herself being lifted outside her body. Not dreaming, but like dreaming. Not watching herself separate and the new part leave the old part, but like that, too.

Eyes do the walking.

That's what.

But not right now.

Through the broad windshield she spied the familiar red and gold lettering in the distance. She held her left arm across her side as if bracing the money against a mild shock. Twisting sideways, releasing her back from the cushion behind her, she pushed off against the seat with her right hand, the force of which was just enough to propel her forward off the bench, a little flight that ended with her standing again at the end of the aisle down which she had made her way fifteen minutes earlier.

The man in the corner of the bench slept on. Just as well. I didn't feel like talking.

Holding the chrome railings at the back of each double seat, she walked forward until she stood beside the rear doors. She shuffled a slow 45-degree angle to her right and faced them, their vertical rubber flaps meeting like grotesque lips, their narrow windows flicking at her images of the shops and street activity she was passing by.

She picked one of the rectangular glass panes, rounded slightly at the corners, and looked through it, making it her private opening to the bustling world she would step down into at the end of the block. Traffic slowed the bus, halting it three times before Delia's stop, before Woolworth's, where she would look for the bird she had decided her life had brought her to, or to which she had come on this trip through it.

When the bus moved, and she tilted first toward the back and then forward and upright again in response to its motion, she focused on the window itself, seeing its beveled edge disappearing into the rubber insulating strip that surrounded it. It was a frame around a picture, stationary as a picture frame should be, but the picture itself swam and streaked and crisscrossed beyond it, a confusing depth of movement that was given changing speeds by the bus's irregular progress.

Then the bus would stop, its air brakes whooshing, and Delia would be put through her tilting in reverse order. While the bus was still she watched people walking purposefully on the wide sidewalk, sunlight patching an awning's lush cover here, green as a forest, there a rack of sausages, never saw so many, dangling inside a delicatessen window, two women bent toward an arm and forefinger extended from them as though they were one body, pointing at a grandfather clock that seemed also to be its reflection, here a man removing his biscuit and raking his arm across his forehead, hat waving to no one, there a tray of onions round, here a mortar and pestle painted on glass.

She liked neither the picture when it was filled with double motion—its own and the bus's—nor the stop tableaus, with nothing really to fix her eyes on and keep her bearings.

Same old rush be going on. Must be like what those little fishes in the Marshall's tank see. Get used to one view, and somebody move it to another table. Somebody sometimes me. Hunh.

She closed her eyes, chuckling to herself, humming and moving her lips in and out over her false teeth. Little spots of light danced on the inside of her lids. Her smile broadened.

They be the dim and flaring lamps.

His righteous sentence.

She was carrying a tray of canapés, including some of those silly sandwiches—Mrs. Marshall loved them—where you cut the bread pieces the same size as the slice of cucumber between them. Troublesome as spreading mayonnaise on the bread was, and putting those little piles together, it pleased her to see the guests have a harder time picking them off the tray than she did making them. She had on the black dress with the white apron that Mrs. Marshall insisted all the help—regular and extra—wear for her parties. The apron was almost big enough to do any good if she spilled something, what with its hanging from the waist ties like a baby's bib. Covering her like a whatchacallit.

Roy had known its name. A charity belt, only another word. She had forgotten.

How can they be dim and flaring at the same time?

Roy squeezed himself into the memory of Mrs. Marshall's party. Delia knew when her mind took trips into the parts of her body Roy used to travel to, his image would rise, just like his wonder weaver used to rise. Lord it was something to see, Roy so proud of it, and something to feel, too, she proud of both of them wrapping around it, loving each other, keeping each other. They would go on and on.

Charity was what they made, so that belt was the opposite. The cruelty of wearing such a harness made a shiver run up her spine, but even the momentary imagined feel of it—cold and metallic against her loins—didn't break her concentration on the constellations sparkling her inner eye, or the man she'd been married to for nine years once.

He's not all gone. He keep showing up inside me.

My righteous sentence.

Roy's image faded, smiling. Her left arm raised itself in the bus, coming to shoulder level, and waved, her hand turning back and forth like Mrs. Marshall's did when she was trying to pull on a fancy glove. Then her arm returned to her side.

She was back at the party. She took the tray with its last few snacks into Mr. Marshall's den, a small room tacked onto the living room, on the other side of the fireplace.

No one was in there, so she walked across the rug to the easy chair in the far corner. She let her small body down gently on the edge of the cavernous indentation Mr. Marshall had embedded over the years in the leather. She rested her tray in her lap.

Reached down, massaging her bunion gently. Party shoes.

And rested herself.

As the tinkling conversation from the other room leaked into her retreat, she looked at the familiar objects surrounding her: low coffee table with its crazed finish, marred by a circle from an old glass someone hadn't set into one of the coasters stacked on the filing cabinet in the corner; the row of three windows to her left, hidden now by the drawn, brocaded drapes, their burgundy color enriched by the floor lamp next to the exposed chimney; the old exterior frame siding Mr. Marshall hadn't covered when the room was built, sliced in two vertically by the brick chimney, two brass ducks in flight across it; Mr. Marshall's glass-topped desk beside her on the right, its chair gone into the other room for the party.

All neat and settled, except for the goldfish tank one of the temporary help had moved from the foyer to the desk. She counted six fish, all versions of each other. There were no strange black ones, taller than they are long, or any of those rainbow, thin kind, either. Just the regular ones.

One of them flitted about more rapidly than the others, weaving among them, suddenly darting down, flicking the bottom and stirring up a tiny trail of dust with its tail as it burst upward again.

What is dust in a fish tank?

Some white growths streamed in the current as the active fish slipped past them, making Delia think of the beauty of the lilies across the sea, which she had never seen. Then the fish, as if ejected from a cannon, spurted toward the top of the tank, leveling off just as it reached the edge of the water; it undulated its body, as if it had been suddenly overcome with cold, swimming in this odd way in zig-zags, its lacy dorsal fin breaking into the air.

Delia picked away specks of white bread from the canapés on her tray and dropped them into the tank. A docile fish zipped up and grabbed at one, while the others among that quiet group stirred slowly and fed on the sodden bits of bread as they sank. But the single fish continued its agitation, apparently not noticing Delia's gift.

Nuff of this lollygaggin. Sposed to be feeding people, and here I am feeding fish.

But she showed no hurry as she rose, straightening her dress and fussing the small apron back into smoothness. O Roy. The busy fish gave up its rigmarole and eased about halfway down the tank, coming to the front edge and seeming to settle there.

Delia bent her knees, the tray in both hands now before her. She and the fish looked at one another briefly, eye to eye, the glass pane between them as monolithic as Moses's tablets bearing God's Thou-Shalt-Nots down from Sinai.

She straightened again, and turned from the fish tank, and the bus lurched to its present stop at Woolworth's corner; she opened her eyes, and the doors spasmed and groaned and flapped apart before her.

To get off she released her stranglehold on the hand grip and turned sideways, letting her left foot down slowly, suspending it a second until her sense of balance caught up with this first stage of her descent. Then the foot thumped the step. She wiggled it out to the edge, making room, and brought the other foot down beside it.

Look at this. I be a crab.

I be sidling.

She repeated the process twice, and stood on the edge of the sidewalk, protected by a lamppost from the crowd surging along beside her.

The bus pulled away, taking with it the throaty roar of its engine, but leaving behind its exhaust fumes, puffy dark deposits thinning into the mid-morning air.

Pew, that what hell can smell like, be too much for me. She shuffled around to face Garner's Market, swiping at the air as if to shoo away a bothersome insect.

Her stomach burbled a little overture in response to the baskets of fresh fruit and vegetables arrayed on tables in front of the market's windows: lemons yellow as jasmine, limes near half as big as oranges, must come from some tropical place, sweet Vidalia onions you could eat like an apple, take a chomp out of it make your mouth water, something the color of a sickle pear but rounder and ugly she didn't recognize, bunches of beets with their greens slung over the edge of the basket like the lank hair of young girls. Her eyes in their luscious fondling of this harvest were suddenly interrupted by a dark form.

Storm cloud.

"Delia?" a voice said.

She brought the level of her gaze to the intimate horizontal, but still couldn't integrate this deep blue solidity that loomed before her.

Can't eat it.

"Delia Walker, you havin a spell? Or what?" Hands waved in front of her. She looked up farther, craning her neck, and watched as a face materialized at the top of the long blue dress, round and brown as a Hershey bar, milk chocolate, scrunched up but grinning.

"You all right?" it said, lips all wiggly as if they had emitted a dozen words instead of three.

Reba Trelette. It was Reba the queen of New Awleen.

"Shure nuff," Delia said. "Whachew think? I was just salivatin on all that produce. Feastin my eyes." She pointed past Reba's elephant-sized purse to Garner's display.

Don't know what's bigger, that cabinet or her mouth. "How you?"

"Lawd, chile, I am overwrought. I could tell you things I've had to endure this morning that would burn your muffins."

And probly will.

"If you had your muffins in the fire." Smirking, Reba poked the knob of Delia's left shoulder, which made her have to resettle her purse strap closer to her own generous neck.

What she tote around in there, anyway?

"The car"—Reba waved her free hand in the direction Delia's bus had come from—"wouldn't start, so I had to suffer the indignity of calling somebody to fix it. I mean, chile, wouldn't you expect . . ."

Delia tried to tune her out, focusing her attention on the side show of Reba's lips, flapping and going out at angles one from the other, then pursing up, only to fall apart like petals off a flower, but she picked up words like "civilized" and "nerve" and "patience."

Reba went on about the difficulty of "securing" a parking place, and the standoffishness of some clerks, and the old refrain she always worked in about wishing she had stayed in Louisiana. Delia wondered how so active a mouth could be set on so stolid a body. Nothing else of Reba Trelette's six-foot frame moved while she talked, not even her hands, except every once in a while to point at, or actually prod, her listener. She was mostly still as a Frigidaire.

Seem like with all that mouth, the body be gyratin around like a dervish.

Reba be tall, too. Really tall.

How tall?

So tall she get four extra hours of light every day.

A silence, the length of which Delia would have been unable to guess at, her attention having finally wandered off entirely, surprised her. She saw Reba's face sharply all of a sudden, the mouth a tamed animal curled in its corner.

"Well?" Reba was obviously waiting for an answer to a question Delia hadn't heard.

"Not much," Delia said. She shifted her feet, stuck out a spindly arm and splayed her fingers against the lamp post. "You know how the white folks is in the spring, with their parties and clubs. It's bout like you can imagine."

Telling Reba she knew, or could imagine, something was usually a sure-fire way of getting her started again. But instead of the "Lawd, chile, don't I" that Delia had already begun to withdraw into expecting, Reba said, "You still cooking for the Marshalls?"

"Un hunh. I am."

"You're not shopping for them on your day off?"

"Naw. Sometimes, but not today." Delia started to tell Reba she had come to town to buy a sparrow, but it seemed too private a thing to have reproduced everywhere Reba went next week. "I'm just pokin around, enjoying the time and the sunshine."

Reba tilted her head as if to peer between Delia's words, or elicit others, but Delia looked past her at the Caribbean limes.

"Well," Reba said. "I'm glad to see you out and about, and not holed up and moping around. Are you really getting along all right by yourself?" A certain edge in Reba's tone made Delia imagine she was tasting the tiny filings around the base of a knife sharpener.

Without Roy, you mean. Whyn't you say it right out? You hide more in yourself than you do in that bag you carry.

I can play, too. Do la de da.

"I find things to"—she put it as she thought Reba might—"occupy me. I keep busy." She aimed her gaze at the bridge of Reba's nose, so Reba would have to go cross-eyed to focus on it. "Memories is wonderful, too. Sometimes it's just like it used to be."

She didn't add *Before you*, but coming to the edge of doing so made her feel like she'd fallen into Reba's trap, or sprung one of her own. Her uneasiness opened into the image of Roy's note on the deal table in the kitchen, waiting for her after a long day at the Marshalls'. Reading it, following his childish printing, his cowardly block capitals marching across the back of the torn envelope, she had felt a stone form in her stomach, growing until it pressed up horribly against her sternum. She had braced herself on the table top and gasped, vowing, even as she wanted to dry up and blow away like the dust thou art, she would not faint. No man, nor no man's walking out, was going to knock her to the floor.

Refuge and strength, she had managed to utter then, barely whispering, her breath taken as by a lick of moonshine, a very present help in trouble, and she found herself now, inwardly quavering before Reba Trelette—the sophisticated stranger who had inserted herself into the lives of decent, God-loving people hereabouts— repeating the same passages from her psalm.

He will not suffer thy foot to be moved.

Until that phrase had come to her as she fought off unconsciousness, and, later, panic and, still later, self-recrimination, she had thought it ridiculous. Why would the Lord God want a person to stand rooted in one place, feet unmoving? Weren't the Israelites wanderers? How could they get to the Promised Land if they didn't go in search of it? But these questions had evaporated when she stood leaning against the table, Roy's note blurred before her.

The Lord will not let me be pushed around.

He will support me in my place.

He will not suffer my foot to be moved.

"Reba," she said, releasing her hold on the lamp post and checking her secret cache with her elbow, "I don't want to keep you from your errands. I know how full up you must be with everything. So I'll say goodbye. Mind how you ago, now."

There was just enough room between the inert obstruction of Reba Trelette and the lamp post for Delia to set her firmly purposeful feet one in front of the other and walk away.

The crowd on the sidewalk parted for her, or seemed to in its fluctuations, and the other people pushing in their pie-slice sections of Woolworth's revolving door made it appear to rotate just for her. Doing a little jig step to keep from being caught and whirled beyond her desire, she popped from it and surveyed the inside of the store.

She had been in Woolworth's often enough to know the main entrance opened into women's clothing, but she never got over how much there was of it, and how it changed every time.

Lot of people somewhere stitching and pedaling overtime to make all this. Wonder what they do with the leftovers.

Today, however, she didn't dawdle among the new spring dresses and Bermuda shorts, but she did stop for a minute by the display of two-piece bathing suits on a raised platform specially built for the occasion. *Suits Modeled at Noon Today—Refreshments* proclaimed a placard hung by a string around a mannequin's neck.

What they gone do with her when the real ones get here?

She tried to imitate the mannequin's smile and felt her jaw give a faint crack. She ran her finger down the cold plaster of the mannequin's calf, making a ring three times around the raised knob simulating an ankle bone.

Suntan their dummies, too. Not a bad paint job, neither.

She grabbed the ankle, her fingers barely encircling half of it. It appeared she might be supporting the life-sized doll, or causing by her fierce grip pain enough to account for the frozen rictus masquerading as a smile on her mouth.

Take a long time in a mighty hot sun to get black as this hand.

She ran the fingers of her free hand (the left one) over the one holding the mannequin. It was a dry touch, a baked-out, desert grazing of the minutely cross-hatched skin.

Look like a lizard.

That's what.

She patted her gripping hand, smiling to herself, full of the secrets of survival, humming. She raised her moving hand, the hand of her exploration and self-approval, and held it between the capturing hand and the fluorescent display lamp beside the mannequin.

"The Lord is a shade upon thy right hand," she said.

My right hand.

If I wanted to I could move your foot. Clean from under you, Missy. Lay you right out.

Her hand grasping the mannequin began to tremble, and Delia released it, resisting the urge to jerk it back as if she'd been burned. Instead, she drew it away slowly, keeping the shape and feel of the ankle until she cupped both her hands ceremonially in front of her waist.

She looked up, past the mannequin's bare midriff, her modest breasts encased in their shiny sea-green cups, the expanse of fake teeth on one of which, she noticed, a flake of paint had been chipped off, and finally to the long tubes of illumination set in rows on the ceiling.

Another psalm said God is a shield and a sun. Didn't it? How could He be both?

Motion beside her, and a thinning of the light around her—.

"Are you looking for something?"

"Birds," Delia said.

"What?"

The clerk leaned toward her, peering over the tops of a pair of pince-nez spectacles. From each ear a miniature chain hung almost to the base of her neck, then made rearward curves, disappearing behind it.

Delia looked at one of the chains. "I want to buy a bird," she said, nudging herself again with her elbow, comforted by the little bulge of currency in her waistband.

"That would be the back of the store, on the left past housewares." The woman pursed more tightly her already prim lips, as if she were trying to make them vanish into themselves.

"Thank you," Delia said. She turned away from the clerk and the bathing-suit dummy and resumed her progress through the store.

She got to the houseware section without further distraction, but once there she stopped frequently to examine various items, checking to see if any new and miraculous device had been invented that would make her work easier. Mrs. Marshall kept the kitchen up-to-date for her, often asking Delia if she needed anything that might be helpful. Delia was grateful for that.

Stuck in with the strainers of all sizes she found a flour sifter that fit her hand better than the one she'd become accustomed to. She squeezed the red, wooden handle against the metal brace parallel to it, repeating the grip she had used on the mannequin's ankle.

That be smooth.

She decided to tell Mrs. Marshall about how effortless this motion was, placed the sifter back on the shelf, nestling it in among the strainers so that it wouldn't draw undue attention to itself. The whole bin of strainers tumbled together seemed a wonderful puzzle of tiny, shining wires crisscrossing among and behind each other into a mysterious depth, repeating themselves like honeycomb, or, depending on how you thought of it, a numberless horde of little holes.

Sifting out the hearts of men.

She picked up the hymn's melody again in her mind, humming, too, smiling at the image of God as a baker, manipulating His version of the sifter she had just tested.

Take a big one, all them hearts.

Emerging from housewares she came upon three wide, low steps, covered in a dull, terracotta-colored version of the grooved rubber on the bus steps. She mounted these as she had those others, getting both feet onto one before she assayed the next.

Rising again.

Ascending.

What they call those psalms.

Brief as the climb was, she found she was out of breath at the top, so she took advantage of the bench set between the elevators to the second floor. She eased her body down.

I oughtn't be this tired. Still, I been standing and walking since I left home. Except for the bus. Stood out there with that Reba too long. That was it.

She rubbed her ankles and, easing her bad foot from her sandal, kneaded the bunion and its adjacent ball. Then she leaned against the hard back of the bench and relaxed as best she could. She was about to close her eyes when she noticed across from her a small boy dressed in a sailor suit playing with a yo-yo.

He did the up-and-down pretty good, but when he tried to shoot it out in front of him the string would collapse and the yo-yo plummet to the floor, bringing the boy down to his knees to retrieve it, as if the gadget were manipulating him instead of the other way round.

Whole load of stuff people thinkin up. And makin. For a second Delia thought her mysterious heaviness was coming on her again, but this time it was a different feeling. The accumulation of the day's perceptions seemed to have peaked in the boy's yo-yo, not in itself the most unusual thing she'd seen, but perhaps the most outlandish. Something about it—perhaps nothing more than the string connecting it to the boy who sought to control its motions—set it apart from the dust swirling in the fish bowl, or the lips of the bus door, or Reba's mouth, or the bountiful fruit spread in front of Garner's, or the mannequin, or even God as the sifter of the universe. Watching the yo-yo arc down through its loop from the boy's fingers, hang suspended by his ankle—

how it do that?

—and rise back into his cupped hand, Delia felt her self shrinking, poising down to the size of a raisin, and the store expanding, like a balloon filling and filling with air. The store became the world, not just all the things she knew and didn't understand, or didn't know and wondered about, not just the inanimate things and animate people she referred to unconsciously when she said *world*—all that other than herself—but the planet itself, the blue globe spinning in the wooden cradle set on a tripod in the Marshall's big living room, in front of the bay window.

It was a momentary vision. When she brought her eyes from the yo-yo ascending once more to the boy's hand, and moved her gaze up his arm to his shoulder and neck and face, she was back to her normal size in the normal Woolworth's, shifting her fanny against the hard bench.

She registered the boy's resemblance to the Marshalls' grandson, and another reverie cushioned her for a moment or two longer against her present discomfort.

He be a strange one, that Mark. All that hair falling on his forehead. Of the large, extended family whose members filtered constantly in and out of her employers' house, he was the only one who came into her kitchen for no other reason than to sit with her. She wondered why he didn't have friends his own age, why he didn't roam around the house behind one or another of the women, or amuse himself in the yard, or at the breakwater. Lots of things for a boy to do around there.

He don't mope exactly. He be inward.

He do love his grandfather, though. Too bad the man can't be home more. But Mr. Marshall did take a longer time for lunch during the week Mark visited each month, she noticed that, and spent his Saturday mornings in the garage where the boy could play, instead of tinkering with the engine in his boat. Ever since the old man had fished him out of the bay, Mark hadn't been allowed on the dock.

Delia remembered that day not so much for the event itself— though she recalled that well enough—as for the way she had connected her image of Mark under water with her puzzlement over why he spent so much time under the dining-room table during meals.

Seem like half the time I come in there he gone under that table again. She had no reasonable explanation for this habit, so she lit on one that made sense to her.

Maybe he like feet.

She wondered what her feet looked like to him. Hers would be the only moving feet, going from chair to chair, shuffling off to the serving table, disappearing and reappearing around that folding Chinee screen at the walk-through to the kitchen. Imagining the boy's attention to her feet gave her a hint of shared life with him, a kind of gentle intimacy that helped her welcome him into her kitchen when he came there.

He see my feet. He see my socks rolled down.

She bent to cozy her sandal back on and noticed the boy in the sailor suit had disappeared.

Gone through the floor.

Yo-yo pulled him through the floor.

I be a crazy old fool, that's the truth.

She nodded her head in assent to her evaluation, placed her right hand on the bench and, pushing and sliding and humming, stood up, unbending slowly.

When she reached her full five-foot-two vertical extension into the Lord's world, and Woolworth's popcorn-scented air, she craned her neck a little, as if to rise an iota higher above the islands of merchandise around her. She didn't see any model birds to match the one she carried in her imagination, but she did fancy she heard chirping sounds.

When she saw the cages ahead of her—six of them hanging on the bowed tops of stands, like floor lamps—she remembered that Woolworth's sold living birds. Maybe she hadn't really forgotten that knowledge, but it had buried itself somewhere in her mind, and when she watched those sparrows the other day it had risen near enough to the surface to move her here, her real purpose unknown to herself. Like those sparrows stopping in the eaves, in the shade, not flying all the way to the ridgepole.

The cages were arranged in an oval with enough space between each one so she could walk all around and see the birds from every angle. A long, rectangular area on the floor, noticeably darker and

less scuffed than the aisles she'd been walking in, suggested one
of the large merchandise bins had been removed to make space for
the birds. Their glinting, brassy cages, the openness which had been
created for them in the square-cornered and claustrophobic setup
of the surrounding part of the store, the circular shape within which
Delia moved, feeling oddly lighter, released from the obstacles to
her search and the thick mesh of time in which she had been
threading it, and the songs of the birds that were now a ground
from which everything else seemed to draw its being—all this made
Delia feel she had stepped into a festivity, like the center ring of a
circus, or the front of the church where the saved gathered to sway
and chant and sow the ecstatic air with hallelujahs.

Be jubilant, my feet.

She let herself perform a little march, weaving in and out among
the cages, completing a round of all six in one direction, and then
reversing herself and going back the other way.

She imagined trailing a golden cord from her right hand, leaving
behind a looping ribbon of brightness connecting the poles from
which the cages hung.

All wound together.

Wings of the morning.

She stopped and looked about. Things continued in their oblivious course: customers scattered here and there pored over this item
or that, clerks rang up sales at the cash registers, the sun caked itself
on the plate glass window at the rear of the store about fifty feet
down from her. No one had noticed her marching on.

Nobody care how crazy I am.

She looked from bird to bird and thought how they didn't know
crazy from turnip greens. Sing and peck all day. Sleep at night?

She realized fleetingly, in a flare of insight that would probably
not last out her time in Woolworth's, that it wasn't other people she
was worried would judge her, it was herself. Along with the image
of the bird she wanted to carry home, to be, and her memories of
Roy, locked in love childless and forever gone, and the Marshalls
whose lives and possessions—the very dust of their lungs—barred
her sense of her everyday being as the shadow cast by the mullions
on one of their windows lay indiscriminately across rug and desk

blotter and doily, she carried around inside her, her own grid of self-judgment. She knew who she was by its coordinates just as clearly as if it were a map of her neighborhood.

It came to her that *this* was what it meant to say you couldn't save yourself. It wasn't sin—she had never felt she was a sinner in the deep, soul-scourging way she had been taught she should feel—that damned you, it was the inescapability of your own judgment of yourself. She needed mercy because she was unable to have mercy on herself.

That be the alien land.

That be the place that requires a song.

The birds' chirping was pushed to the periphery of Delia's hearing by the deeper voice of another clerk asking if she needed assistance.

"I want to buy one of these birds," she said.

"Which one?" The clerk peered down at her with a mixture of amusement and concern playing on his face.

Delia looked closely at the birds, seeing them individually for the first time. Five of them were versions of each other: parakeets, colored variously, but in shape and tilt of head and general carriage very much alike. Her heart danced at the sight of them all, but her eye finally settled on the sixth one, a compact canary whose color seemed a pure feathering of sun and butter.

Flying light.

She walked over and stood close to the cage. The canary flitted from the high perch it had been balanced on to the lower one on Delia's side of the cage. The small, forty-seven-year-old black woman and the smaller yellow bird looked one another in the eye.

The bird cocked its head.

Delia cocked hers. Smiled. She raised her forearm, pivoting at the elbow—a slow and reserved gesture such as a monarch might have made singling out to a trusted retainer a subject to be given special favor—and pointed at the canary.

"How much is that one?"

The clerk walked around the outside of the circle to the other side of the cage and flipped over a tag hanging from one of the bars. "Seven dollars and seventy-five cents." He enunciated the numbers as if he were talking to a child, as if the sounds coming from his mouth were little blocks of wood whose edges he was shaving off.

The canary chirped at Delia, and reversed its perch on the dowel. Show me your whole self.

"I'll be back in a minute," Delia said to the clerk's chin, which looked to her like a shelf sliding uninterrupted from his lower lip to the knot of his tie.

She shuffled past some garden tools to the side where she knew a staircase descended to a place customers couldn't go. She went down three steps, turned toward the wall and tucked her chin down into her chest. In a series of quick, furtive maneuvers that made her body look from above as if it were palsied, she extracted the folded bills from the waistband of her underwear.

She straightened and slipped the money into her pocket beside her change purse. When she had buttoned her top button and shifted until, mirrorless, she was satisfied her dress was smoothed and hanging properly, she climbed back to the sales floor.

The clerk, who had started walking toward the stairwell, stopped abruptly when she emerged from it. But he retained his expression of indignation, radiating implicit disciplinary action from his pursed lips.

"I needed some privacy," Delia said.

Didn't do nothing.

The clerk's face relaxed a bit, and so did Delia.

But she still had a problem.

"I only got six dollars." She passed the bills to the clerk, one at a time, laying each in his outstretched hand, counting in a whisper, hoping somehow an extra dollar she had failed to separate out would reveal itself.

"Six," she mumbled, and her giving hand hovered a second beside the fluff of bills lying on the clerk's palm. She lowered it to her side.

"Do you have a charge account with us?"

What kind of question is that? Not even the king of Africa get a charge account here.

She shook her head, but she looked the clerk in his flighty little eyes.

He will not suffer thy foot to be moved.

The canary ran off a trill of music that gave her goose bumps. Over the clerk's sloping shoulder she saw it hop to the higher perch again.

"Wait a minute," the clerk said. "Aren't you the girl who works at the Marshalls'?" He went through a pantomime of examining Delia's face. "Why, yes, I believe you are. It's Delia, right?"

Before Delia could say anything one way or another the clerk had zipped over behind the cash-register desk, run his forefinger down a list of names and numbers beside the wall phone, and was busy dialing one of them.

Girl!

Delia realized what he was up to, but when she arrived at the edge of the desk, her indignation at what the man had called her and her shame at what he was doing, one emotion struggling with the other, rendered her speechless.

She opened her mouth, but the only sounds she heard were the phone being replaced in its cradle, and, behind her, another joyous lilt from the canary.

"Mrs. Marshall is quite happy to guarantee the other one dollar and seventy-five cents. I'll write that up."

Delia let her lips settle against each other again. A thousand dots of dry heat prickled her face, feeling like they came from the air in the store, and at the same time rose up from her throat and through the roof of her mouth. The bridge of her nose felt heavy and compressed, as if a stone wanted to be delivered from it. Her feet tingled. Her bones hollowed out and her skin lightened, ready to flake off and blow away.

She wanted to blow away altogether, disintegrate right there into the dust thou art, and be borne off on the wind.

But the clerk and canary intervened again, as if from opposite and irreconcilable extremes they were conniving to save her from the very predicament they were also at the center of.

"Make your mark here," the clerk said, and the bird uttered a diminutive, parrotlike shriek that sounded to Delia like laughter.

She remained silent. She felt solid and cool again. She adjusted the thick pad the clerk had set on the counter before her, turning it so the angle suited her. Taking up the pen lying beside the charge pad she signed her name —*Delia H. Walker*—as if she were an artist signing a painting.

It was a signature with no quiver in it.

She laid the pen down, turned, and walked to the canary's cage. The bird was silent, too, waiting with Delia to go home.

I pay her back.

It be my money in the end.

Girl.

She endured the clerk's instructions about feeding—a free packet of seed accompanies all avian purchases at Woolworth's—hygiene —I'm putting the instruction sheet in the cage for your convenience; don't leave it there—and cage placement. He removed the cage from its hook on the floor stand, holding it by the base.

Delia hooked her finger into the golden ring the cage's bars arced into, and bore it away from the oval of birds through which she had marched her twining kinship a few minutes ago. That elation had settled now, filtered and strengthened by shame and anger, and she felt like she and the canary were old friends heading together toward a familiar destination.

I let you loose sometimes.

He watch you, don't need to be a sparrow.

I've had my going out. Now for the coming in.

In her mind she was already through the revolving doors, lifting her foot, beginning her ascent into the curved stairwell of the bus, holding the cage aloft like a lantern.

Mariah

M A R I A H   A D V E N T   had never considered herself a practical
Christian. She wasn't sweet, or charitable, or patient. She didn't
cross the road to help her neighbor, or give her coat to a shivering
pilgrim, for one of them would still be coatless. She did not turn
the other cheek, if by *cheek* one meant a part of her face. But she
had turned the *other* other cheek frequently in her time.

And not a bad set of cheeks, either, to sheathe in a pair of tights,
and move proudly in the world among those not blessed with such
suppleness. She had turned *heads* frequently in her time, too.

Turned them, and given good measure for their turning when
she chose.

This morning, though, she sat on the edge of the double bed, not
feeling the mattress sag slightly, or the edge of the collage she had
worked on so long crinkle under her. Between the rippled side of the
bleached shade and the window frame sunlight sprayed, glancing
off one of the big brass knobs on the bedstead and gilding a section
of the wallpaper: brown roses, a few now sunflecked, dotting a
butternut background.

She saw none of this, however, nor the shadow her own body
had begun to throw over the golden center of the collage spread
behind her.

Normally it would have been her day off, Saturday, and she would
have spent it meditating, which in the past had meant nothing

systematic or programmed according to a religious regimen of any kind, Eastern or Western. Mariah's meditating day had been composed of keeping her body occupied with various domestic projects so her mind could release itself into the mansions of air denied it during the week. Working salads, and keeping freshly stocked the trays on the long line at the cafeteria, gave her neither time nor energy for her soul's health, though not long ago, when she began drawing, that had altered significantly.

She had taken the job across the street from the shopping center —so new not all the store spaces had been rented yet—because she had thought the work would afford her a chance to unshackle her meditative life from its Saturday confinement and spread it over the whole week.

She had imagined her hands in mountains of lettuce, seeing the droplets of water pop upward as she broke open the clumps of it, revealing the paling green inwards of the smaller leaves hugging themselves. She had felt the almost furry tops of broccoli forests against her fingers, breaking the larger bunches down into little flowers, and the rougher, less giving brain mounds of cauliflower. Slicing beets and tomatoes, cucumbers and bell peppers—she had always wanted a dress the deep, hypnotic green of a pepper—her arms and wrists and hands and fingers engaged with these cool fruits of the earth had seemed to promise her a rote intimacy from which her thoughts could fly into the hidden shapes of her enlightenment.

Oddly enough, the job she had left to go to the cafeteria had given her too *much* time to herself, too many stretches where she had nothing to do. *Leisure time* she heard it called on the radio; a person nowadays had more of it than ever before, because of modern conveniences that cut down the time formerly needed to get the basic chores of a household done. And this was true. Her job as cook and maid at the Randoms' had been daily proof of it. The dishwasher washed the dishes; the disposal ground up the kitchen waste so there was little garbage to tote out to the big can in the alley. Even the sheets were presewn to fit snugly around the mattress corners, so smoothing the one bed she had to make was a snap.

But it felt wrong. It was as if the center of something had been removed and the outer parts abandoned to an increasingly vacuous whirling, a wheel turning without an axle. Once, sitting in the kitchen while the pressure cooker steamed vegetables and the oven timed a roast, she had imagined a planet lose its axis and go fluttering off without control, gradually fraying at the edges, dispersing parts of itself into space, tatters of a scarecrow's rags, until it spread so thin it disappeared. The experience had excited her at first, seeming to be an instance of the very meditation she sought, but she had also been unsettled—even frightened—by the particular way her feeling had embodied itself. If this was the direction in which leisure time cast her inner thoughts, she wanted no more of it. In spite of the generous raise old Mr. Random had offered her, and the amiable way he and his sweet wife treated her, she had given two weeks' notice and filled out an application for the cafeteria opening.

How could she explain to Mr. Random that his proposal to rearrange her duties so she would have more time for herself would have only made things worse? As it was, Mrs. Random fried chicken herself because her husband wouldn't eat anyone else's. The only time Mariah really enjoyed her six months with the elderly couple was their July Fourth dinner for their relatives.

They had come from all over, including as far away as Arkansas and Florida, and as close as two blocks over in Tergin Park where the Randoms' sons lived, all within a mile of each other. Mariah had worked for all of them at one time or another, filling in when their help got sick, or lending a hand at parties and local family gatherings, usually on Sundays. They each had children, too, nine altogether, a hodge-podge of grimy, loud energies spinning about interchangeably.

Except for one. Mariah remembered how one of the grandsons, Mr. Random's son's son—Seth was it? Most of them had funny, one-syllabled names, names with no music in them, so when you said them it sounded like you were whining or barking or coughing: Jane and Hank and Mark—Mark, that was the one. Seth was his father. She had heard old Mr. Random's standard joke about how hard it was to keep everybody straight anymore, there were so many, and the more arrived the worse his memory got. He had hired somebody to fill out the family tree as far back as he could dig, but had told him never mind when he found out an immediate forbear had been

a corporal in the Confederate army who had deserted to sell mules
to both sides.

She remembered how Mark had closed the oven door on her
when she was substituting at the son's house. Hovering around the
kitchen like he'd emerged from the wall or might vanish into it at
any minute. Couldn't have been more than five or six years old. Not
saying anything. Mariah had wondered if he was just interested in
what she was doing, which at that moment was baking rolls.

"They're not quite brown enough," she said, glancing from the
rolls to the boy and back. "See?"

He approached and, standing beside her, bent toward the four
cast-iron pans out of which puffed twenty-four nearly lighter-than-
air caps of homemade bread.

"Aren't they gems?" Mariah smiled at him.

Instead of answering, or even looking at her, the boy had put
both hands under the door and brought it abruptly up as Mariah
slid the rack back in the oven, trapping her right arm momentarily
in the hot interior. She'd been unable not to cry out, though she
hadn't been burned. A little sun of fear and surprise burst in her
eyes, seeming to her as if the true location of this widening bud of
flame had been inside her forehead—and she dropped the hot pad
in the stove. The only injury turned out to be a bruise on her forearm
where she bumped it when she jerked free of the heat, knocking the
oven door open again. It had bounced, she remembered, flapping
on its hinges, making a noise like one of the Randoms' names.

The boy disappeared. His mother made a fuss, but even as Mariah
was telling her it was nothing, the woman was retreating toward the
bustle of people in the living room, tinkling their glasses in the pre-
dinner haze of cigarette smoke and bourbon.

She remembered less the boy than the bright blossom in her
head, and after that the phrase *lend a hand*—a favorite of old
Mr. Random—had acquired an overtone she would have preferred
to forget.

There had been so much to do for that July Fourth reunion that
she had become engrossed beyond her desire. A week of prepara-
tion, and the unending day of the festivities themselves, had freed
her deepest flights. She had lost track of time in the rising and

widening of vision; while her hands kneaded dough or chopped scallions or speared cloves into the plump hams, and her body adapted itself to the postures of bending and sidling and lifting, her spirit had found shapes it settled in and abandoned—the smell of a flower, or a butterfly lost in a field and suddenly fluttering up, seeming to lift the whole expanse of grass and blossom with its rising. She had flown with a Tuskegee airman, sort of a ghost co-pilot, on a dangerous mission covering a bombing run to central Germany. The silent puffs of exploding anti-aircraft shells—she knew the name for that, *flak,* a word that seemed itself an explosion, the sound of an atmosphere—interspersed with spurts of fire from the guns of another word she remembered from the newspapers years ago, *Messerschmitts,* as many consonants clustered as there were bullets spewing from the wings of the plane. In the midst of this turmoil she noticed the pilot had disappeared; the seat beside her was as empty as a grounded bird's nest in February. As the plane began to veer and plummet she struggled with it, righting it, feeling herself not merely at ease with the controls but drawing from them into her hands and arms the buoyancy of the air, being herself lifted within the little craft she lifted out of the flak and enemy assault toward other explosions—bursts of light above her, and then surrounding her beyond the stratosphere, starwheels and novae and, far off to her looming horizon, the searwhite roil of the sun.

She had stood in the crowd carpeting the ground in front of the Lincoln Memorial. Martin Luther King was telling her about his dream. *I have a dream, too,* her mind replied. She watched the afternoon brightness bank off the white marble of the monument, a sheet of paper peeling from a ream, riding the air, a background against which King's tilting, passionate head took on the dark glow of glory.

She had joined the men in Julian Binford's *The Crapshooter,* watching the dice describe their crazy jigging across the blue plane that was supposed to be the solid surface she tossed the dice on, but appeared a receptive opacity, a pool of aquamarine opalescence, a sky. She had finally fallen into it, or through it into something else. Though she had pitched forward, following her arm as if the dice she released had pulled her by invisible threads attached to her fingers, once she passed into the mysterious skypool she had fallen upward, rising through the cloudlike softness toward a shimmering coalescence of light above her.

She had stood in a battle line, one of thousands of soldiers in blue and gray, helping her brothers and sisters defend their homeland. The enemy amassed a charge against her position, roaring over the ridge line and descending upon her. She raised her musket. Sighting down it, she saw the faces of those looming up toward her cluster, as if to become a better target, drawing together into a flower for her to fire on. She pulled the trigger and the faces ignited from the center of the corona they composed, the flames flaring outward, consuming them wholly.

As her visions faded, she would for an instant watch the gesture in the midst of which she had caught her body, to which in a palpable sense she was returning: seeing her arms spangled with suds from the dishpan they drew a saucer from, or feeling her shoulders tense with the effort of extracting a stack of plates from the lower reaches of the sideboard, or smelling the rich pecans and Karo in the pies she carried to the card tables on the porch.

She quickly discovered that the imperial routines at the cafeteria were no family reunion. Her fantasies about the sensual pleasure of preparing and serving—in this case, keeping the self-service trays and cylinders abundant and appealing—fruits and vegetables, and, she learned, ham and American cheese and diced turkey, not to mention Jell-O and nut and cream-cheese concoctions named after exotic Pacific islands (*salad* had swollen to embrace a multitude of ingredients): those fantasies had proven accurate. But she had not had even the gentlest grazing of vision beckon her. The sameness of her duties numbed her before the first week ended. She dragged herself into bed that Friday, too tired to sleep, a zombie in her white uniform with the red rooster on its breast pocket. She stared at the ceiling. Darkness collected, and soon passing cars flipped their lights from wall to wall. She missed the old couple. She realized what she wished for was some compromise between the undemanding, lapse-dotted days she had spent with them, and the unrelenting and unvarying pressure at the cafeteria. That Fourth of July had been an aberration, an islanded gift to remind her thereafter of the possibilities winging her spirit. But the wide sea of daily life, she knew, seldom offered such landfall.

She began to read the classifieds every day during her thirty-minute lunch "hour," and to watch for posters and other ads in the store windows she passed walking home. Ten weeks after starting her search for another job, she had mostly given up; at first in desperation and then in a kind of resignation that had a hopeful feel about it, like the kernel inside a peach seed, she had developed a ritual for her day off. It was a ritual in outline only, however. She planned to be busy, to engage her body's attention, but beyond that to proscribe nothing. No Saturday, beyond the broad command of physical occupation, would be like another. The exact activities, and their progression, would unfold spontaneously, a living dream with its own logic, one piece connected to the next as surely as a hook into an eye, but without conscious preconception.

A month ago she had been sitting on the floor hunched toward the wide baseboard in her bedroom, picking paint from the grooves lining its crown. She had removed all the paint she could with chemical stripper from the hardware store in the shopping center. It had taken five gallons for the small room, two less than there were coats of paint on the old wood. The only way to get the final dots and slivers that had found niches in the wood to settle in was to gouge them out with the point of a paring knife. Or her ice pick.

It was perfect work. What had at first seemed a disadvantage—stiffness in her back when she bent to do her miniature mining—turned into a boon. She figured out various reclining positions in which she could pick comfortably, and imagined, or felt, as the morning extended itself, that each change of posture was part of a slow, choreographed routine she was performing. She moved clockwise. To her left along the edge of the baseboard little flecks of paint, mostly cream and faded yellow, trailed after her like cosmic dust in a starfall.

In the midst of a like trail of associations in her mind she had remembered Serena Peoples in the vegetable aisle of the Safeway, telling her about the big house where she did cleaning. More rooms than your heavenly mansion itself, she had told Mariah. Even the rooms have rooms, like they reproduce in the dark. Mariah had laughed with Serena at this, but uneasily, for the image of procreating darkness was familiar to her from the edges of some of her visions, and she always turned away from it, though at times it meant a withdrawal from her transport. Serena had said her employers had names for all those rooms. Some after colors—the blue room and like that—and some after their children, only one of whom—there were six—still lived in the palace, as she referred to it. Others had names of battles from The War—Serena came down icily on the two syllables; she couldn't pronounce those and wished she'd never asked Mr. Bowers what they meant, because he had commenced a lecture that went on and on.

Mariah had begun to have a similar reaction to Serena's length-ening list, and had almost tuned herself into the rhythms of the sentences and out of their words, when Serena said *drawing room*. It was nothing to her but another stage in her story, but it struck Mariah. She had paused in her selection of red potatoes, as if to store this phrase securely for future access when she had the appropriate context for it.

That context occurred—though Mariah had forgotten the train of thought that had chugged into the station—as she was lost in dislodging paint the following Saturday.

Her hand had stopped, the ice pick poised above a little well of dead yellow, much as her hand had hovered over the potato bin. It was her turn of mind to *see* what words described—to take them literally—and to entertain, usually with delight, the layers of mean-ing phrases often carried with them unintentionally. Though some-times phrases—like Serena's darkly reproductive rooms—would lead her into more thorny places. She had been undone for a week once by having to untangle *all your waking life*.

Drawing room, however, occasioned first a childlike enjoyment. She imagined a cartoon in which a room, equipped with arms and legs, was able to draw. It created fish for ponds and seagulls for beaches, trees for girls to climb and swings for boys to swing in. It even drew a large, beautifully appointed room for itself to live in, furnished with a draftsman's table for it to draw on—another drawing room.

Having reached that point she let the first depiction fade, and saw herself in the drawing room, the room to draw in (to withdraw to), standing before the table with a long feathered pen in her hand, its sharp point hovering above a brilliantly blank expanse of paper.

The pen faded, too, as it descended, Mariah's conscious attention returning to the ice pick, which she needled into the edge of a spot of recalcitrant paint. As she dug gently, she had decided to make herself a drawing room. It wouldn't be a *room*, of course. She had only two, plus the kitchenette and bathroom. She would rearrange the bedroom—put the bed jam up against the far wall, move the table into the sitting room, hang a gooseneck light over the headboard—and create a space to draw next to the window.

Even before she had agreed with herself about this adjustment, she had realized she didn't have to limit herself to drawing. About this time, too, she had had a vision different in its overall feel and tonality from those she was accustomed to. She thought of it more as a dream, for it had come at night as she lay in bed, doing nothing. She had thought she was asleep at first, but the experience had a waking dimension that made her doubt her precise relationship to it. It was brief, hardly more than a vignette, but vivid and sharp, as if it were etched on her eyeballs. She saw a set of concentric rings, becoming brighter as they approached the smallest zero at the center, which was where she was. She *was* the center, the bull's-eye of this target of gathering brilliance. That was all. Except she knew the archer about to release his arrow of light was Jesus, and he was aiming at her. Over the succeeding four weeks two dimensions of her life noticeably altered.

All the spaces in her apartment opened to her new pursuit; the apartment itself became a drawing room. Whenever she cooked she had to remove from the stove a set of drying brushes, or trays starred with cracked, unused watercolors. Before she could flop on the bed after a day at the cafeteria she spent a few minutes laying in the corner next to the closet the scraps of paper she had pieced out on the spread that morning, to test color or shape combinations. Paper of various sizes and hues draped over her sagging couch, the two cane-bottom chairs and the old pine table she ate off of. Pencils, brushes and drawing markers, pairs of scissors and artists' knives, littered the floors. She did her experimenting and practicing wherever she took a notion to.

The one neat spot was the corner next to the window in the bedroom, the original drawing room. Its focal object was the table Mariah had rigged to work on. She had found two identical end tables at the junk shop around the corner. *Two Balls* the store was called, as was its owner—an obese man whose pudgy little fingers had played on Mariah's arms and shoulders and back like she was a piccolo—because the pawnshop emblem hanging over its recessed doorway lacked a third of the usual equipment. By the time Mariah got out of there, the leering proprietor holding the screen for her, she was sure the designation advertised a personal service as well.

She stacked one end table on the other, and on top of them she angled a piece of plyboard, four feet by four feet, by nailing the near edge on one-inch blocks and the edge turned toward the wall on five-inch ones. These blocks she had first nailed to the top of the second end table. Finding the upper table had a tendency to slide, she had fastened an L-brace to each leg and anchored them to the top of the lower table.

She kept the table dusted, and ran the carpet sweeper in the corner late every evening. The drawing—she adopted the generic term for all her projects—she was focused on at any particular time lay on the slanting board; the supplies she anticipated needing she arranged in rows on the top of the undertable, as she called it. She thought of the two tables in various ways—as the undertow and the waves, or the viscera and the mind, or the undersoul and the oversoul—all determined by their vertical relationship. She saw herself sometimes in a medieval tower, sometimes at the top of a skyscraper, sometimes on a mountainous crag. Accompanying all these aspiring images— their soul, as it were—was Mariah's sense that the structure she worked with had become a person, an identity standing before her, its absolute stillness both a dependence and an offering drawing her outward and deepening her at once.

Time was the other dimension she had reconstructed. The hours she had spent buying equipment, and setting up the drawing table, had disconcerted her. The activity had delayed the moment she could settle in and begin making the pictures and assemblages which had unconsciously stirred as soon as Serena Peoples had uttered the fateful *Sesame*. As much as Mariah enjoyed the little art shop next to the hardware store, buying brushes and special pencils she never knew existed before her need for them, she was impatient with the practical requirements it represented. She learned here, too, the word—*collage*—for plans that already roiled in her mind, and she found, under pressure from both her purse and her imagination, that she didn't have to *buy* most of what she envisioned as pieces in her compositions.

She started collecting posters from the trash piles behind the stores in the shopping center, planning to use the reverse sides, but discovering as she worked that fragments of words and designs sometimes suited her purpose, too. Other employees at the cafe (a short, hard word she liked because it was pronounced like a baby cow) brought her scraps of wrapping paper and leftover sewing material; one of the women who prepared entrees, a sullen, whiplike person who never spoke to anyone, brought her a stack of actual watercolor pads she said her daughter would never use. Serena had swiped two shining Exacto knives and a set of blades from a tool room no one ever entered in the palace.

All of this occupied time, but it was Mariah's actual work that transformed it.

Perhaps her release from unfelt pressure to have her visions while she was at the cafeteria caused the change; perhaps the daily anticipation of her life outside the salad division; or the removal of the barrier between physical and visionary energy: whatever the cause, her hours at the cafe passed quickly, even with a sort of enjoyment in the rhythms of the work and her developing rapport with some of the other employees.

She came home as fresh as if she'd just awakened from the rejuvenating sleep of a fairy tale. She ate her chicken or ham sandwich, holding a glass of milk in the other hand, moving from bedroom to living room to kitchen, surveying the scraps and partial assemblages spread about like wildflowers in a meadow. Some evenings she would get no further than this ambulatory rumination, adjusting a piece of one grouping or adding color to the edge of an abstract scene daubed on the back of a poster. Other days brought

heightened intensity to the central project atop the oversoul. Whatever her focus, she worked regardless of time, a presence moving
among her material as if it were pieces of herself she was drawing
together into a transcendent singularity.

Over the next couple of months she felt she had accomplished
this frequently. A round dozen collages—ranging in size from three
feet by five feet to six by six—hung in a row around the living-room
walls, a growing environment. The irony of having to continue—of
going on to another collage after she had seemed to assemble and
garner the heart of illumination in the one she had just finished—
wasn't lost on her. She spent Saturdays cleaning the apartment,
absorbed in domestic chores, collecting the plates and glasses from
the floor and chair arms and the side of the tub, making the rest
of the place look as good as the drawing room always did, and
drawing back from herself to consider where she was in her quest.
She sensed that not knowing what she sought was an indispensable
dimension of the search itself, and rather than being troubled or
frustrated by this she was energized instead.

Two weeks before, scrubbing the bathroom floor, drawing the
brush in rhythmic arcs across the small black-and-white tiles, feeling
the suds tingle as they evaporated on the left hand and forearm
which bore her leaning weight, her neck and shoulders rolling
gently with the brush, she had had a breakthrough.

As she scrubbed she envisioned Jesus on the cross, not once but
twelve times, the repeated crucifixions making a circle on the crest
of a hill. She always imagined Jesus as having skin the same light
brown as her own, with an undertone tending vaguely toward olive,
but this Jesus, all twelve of him, was stark black, with the deepest
possible blue glowing from within. His head hung to the right, as
if it wanted to nestle against his own shoulder. Though they never
actually moved, his eyes were closing, in spite of the rigid, two-inch
strands of wire stuck vertically through them into his cheek bones.
The cast of the whole man was sorrowful; he was pulled toward the
earth, not as if gravity wanted to drag him off the cross but as if he
was being drawn *through* it, or merged with it, into one being.

Mariah's body, on all fours except for the arm wielding the brush,
had begun to sway and dip, and little moans escaped her lips, parted

as if to whisper some impending secret. Her experience of the vision split into two perspectives: she watched simultaneously from above, seeing the circle composed by the twelve kinky-haired heads of Jesus atop their severely foreshortened bodies, and from a vantage an inch from the eyes of one Jesus, although she knew the eyes of the others burned with the same fury, making a white speck in their deepest centers. These two perspectives merged slowly as the circle tightened, gradually becoming a black dot—one head coalesced from twelve—which superimposed itself over the burning core of the eye of Christ. The aura of the fire around the compressed black dot looked like an eclipse of the sun for an instant, and then the depth of the white heat consumed the black coal and a brilliance beyond relief or forbearance spread to the edges and plunged to the bottom of Mariah's vision.

She uttered an O, her secret and revelation, no louder or more forceful than the series of moans which had preceded it, and her body, without twitch or seizure, rolled gently on its side, letting the brush rest untended on its bristles against the tile.

When she woke she gathered herself and sat on the lip of the tub. She brushed the right side of her work dress, damp from the floor. She rubbed her forehead; she made little circles with her fingers against her temples. Then she eased herself back to the tiles, dipped the brush in the bucket and began scrubbing again.

She brought two discoveries from the vision. She would change the basic shape of her collage backing from the rectangle to the circle. And the controlling image she sought would become a blossom of fire.

This shift proved to be more difficult than she expected. In fact, as she removed the rectangular collages from the walls and disassembled them, salvaging everything including the anchor joints where four or five layers of material had been spot-glued over each other, she expected no difficulty at all. It was a matter of knowing better what she was doing, a sharper fix on purpose and design, a deeper connection of her soul's drive and its embodiment in the world.

What surprised her—unsettled her in the same way the images of darkness multiplying itself had—was the sudden recurrence of sexual memories from the part of her life she had thought was over.

The drawing room had led her, she thought ruefully, to the dark room. She knew she would have to unpin the prints hanging from the strings there, to look at the frozen images by the light of day.

At first only isolated scenes intruded: a sweaty man on a bed watching her peel off her underwear in the glow from a dim red light; standing above a cluster of crapshooters, feeling their frank glances crawling up the mini-skirt she taunted them with, knees apart; smoking a cigarette, alone at a table in some ramshackle road house at three A.M., not even the drunk piano player outlasting her.

The lurid quality of these disjunct images stunned her. She had cast herself in bad movie roles—stereotypes —as a way of reducing herself; she knew the harshness of the evaluation shaping her memories wasn't appropriate to the things she had done, but that knowledge wavered like a mirage in the desert when she realized, as well, she had no access to what had really happened except through the screen of judgment.

The pride she had taken in her body and its spontaneous skills, the pleasure that had spilled her so often over the edge, the wide, nitty-gritty, slow-motion fall into sparkle, the miracle of friction issuing in silk—all this was confused and diminished, skewed by disgust and repulsion. She had no way of telling if she had suppressed this sense of crassness and thinned humanity during those abandoned years, or if she had unconsciously developed the perspective in the time since, a filter through which she projected her memories.

In a few days, the frequency and extension of such scenes multiplied. No coherence connected them other than Mariah's self-laceration; no person appeared more than once to give her a figure on which to shift her burden, to ease her blame by sharing it. The gradual increase in the number of scenes seemed a sexual experience itself, as if each specific memory were a stroke in her, deeper and swifter and more lubricious, the sequence stimulating her toward some final focus that would explode and release like orgasm.

Even in the growing anticipation of this, she admitted to herself—more by accretion than by sudden understanding—that, for all their sweetness and elation, sometimes brutal, her orgasms had never transported her in the same way her friends recounted theirs. Giving them the leeway of hyperbole, of their need for self-elevation, Mariah never felt she quite apprehended the ecstasy they described. Without their standard to measure against, she suspected she would still feel a vague disorientation, as if while walking on a path which appeared clear before her, she had snagged her skirt on a thorn.

And there had always been that distance in which she had watched herself, a bird on a wire. Until someone had told her how she just shot loose of the universe, fell apart in the stars, or spread into the light of the world, Mariah had thought being a spectator at her own coming was a normal part of the experience. After a while she concluded that, for her, it was. For all her friends' wild fables of melting into the deep lava—which she neither believed nor disbelieved, but loved for the rich appeal of their speech—she made no effort to change her way of drawing the groove to a climax.

So she was not surprised when the insistence of her memories began to fade, their frequency to diminish, the process reversing itself until, after a few days of random disruptions similar to the cinematic blips the whole series had started with, they disappeared altogether.

She realized that this two-week rush of memory recapitulated the course the years of her sexual life had followed. She had begun by experimenting, moved more by curiosity than lust—though she knew that beneath every stage of every entanglement she was searching for someone to love her wholly, to whom she would give herself without stint—and had gradually involved herself as an addict with a drug, testing the fine and deadly edges of all its illusory rapture. Then she withdrew. There had been no addiction. The bird on the wire called its image back into itself and flew away. The ease with which Mariah had extracted herself was not matched, however, by those people from whom she had walked away. Men sought her out, strangers and cast-offs alike, taking her explanations and denials—which grew more terse and rankling with the passing weeks and months—as just new routines of seduction and foreplay. They understood her various forms of refusal as merely covering her willingness, her yearning, much as they saw their limp foreskins as a momentary disguise over the hard proof of desire that always emerged from them.

She had cut most of that off finally by moving to the neighborhood she currently lived in, though it was shrinking, the result of urban "improvement." The shopping center where she worked sprawled over land where many of her acquaintances once carried on their lives. Yet, even now, fifteen years after the cajoling and wheedling and cursing had begun to die off—her reputation becoming a legend as separate from her as a discarded dress—she had to fend off an occasional pass.

During the period of her memories' disruption she had accomplished very little with her art, but when it was over she renewed her daily immersion; it was not that she came again to her new vision as if nothing had happened, but as if she had brought decision into what had been an accidental phase of her life. The sequence of memories struck her now as an invitation to reenter what she had passed through, to take up a way of living she had drifted into and out of. She had endured the compressed version of her past with impatience, feeling intruded upon by another person, and had with relief and gladness repudiated it. The release she enjoyed was enhanced by her rejection of the tawdry judgment the memories had come wrapped in. She knew that whatever had caused that perspective was as dead now as the alien woman who had carried it inside her.

Once she started to draw and cut and shape again, further changes, fundamental as they were, went unnoticed. She began to forget to change the sunflower seeds or the bread sticks at work, or someone would have to remind her to eat her lunch (which some days she neglected to pack, meaning she had to eat cafe food), or an odd color or shape on the tray line would suddenly register on her eye and she would turn to find she'd put out two bins of lettuce and omitted something else. Two Fridays she missed dates for supper with Serena, not realizing it either time until Serena dropped by later to see if she was sick.

At home she would perform her Saturday-morning rounds of the apartment—now a studio—and find no dishes to wash, or at best a plate or two whose surfaces the mice had polished so thoroughly she put them back on the shelf.

These incidental ticks were signs of a more fundamental shift. Her old way of releasing herself through physical labor—especially when it spread sensual contentment through her body, as preparing vegetables did—for the visions that promised her spiritual fulfill-ment, underwent a reversal. After she witnessed Jesus draw himself twelvefold into a coal, which he then consumed in the fire of his own eye, she lived in and for her visions. She let the exterior world fade, paying no attention to the messages of its former appeal which her senses still tried to relay to her.

She did notice, but only barely, as one notices the presence of an insect in the next room, that her eyesight was deteriorating. She developed small shimmers of opacity, a kind of beige glare, in the centers of both eyes, which she had to look around in order to gauge color and shape for her collages. She would cock her head, resembling a robin searching the ground, and view everything from her periphera.

Her visions changed, too, or their locations did. They didn't come *to* her now, as visitations entering her the way guests came to call; they resided *in* her, and sought instead to be released and given exterior shapes. No, not shapes, but *a* shape, a single incarnation en-compassing the intractable extremes of darkness and brilliance, of compression and release, of depth and height, she had become part of that Saturday as she lay moaning gently on the bathroom tiles.

So she roved her studio, an extension in all directions of the focus of her central assemblage, itself moved to the bed since the surface of the makeshift double table was no longer big enough for the scale on which Mariah engaged her conception. The edges of the circular backing spilled over the bed, which she had pulled away from the walls, rising slightly over the head and foot boards. This was the foundation piece, burgundy poster board she had glued together, whose darkness she had deepened and thickened with repeated washes of Prussian blue and forest green, eventually applying the paint in thick blobs she spread about with a kitchen knife. Unadulterated colors no longer satisfied her. She ravaged the trash bins at the shopping center, her head tilting side to side, often in the early mornings. One day a city trash truck blared its Klaxons at her. She raised herself from the stack of flattened brassiere cartons she had been bowed to and found herself surrounded by noon: she was supposed to be at the cafeteria.

A panel of velvet black covering for ad boards gave her the final dimension of richness she needed for the backing circle— the sphere of heads and one head, the farthest cup of the galaxies, the deepest cave of the earth. She spent a week on the living-room floor cutting the material into minutely narrow strips that she carried one by one, like offerings, into the bedroom and embedded into the miniature ranges of paint that had given the burgundy paperboard the appearance of a relief map. Looking at the result as a dawn filtered through her bedroom window, she saw its light fall effortlessly forever into the subtle gradations of midnight she had blended, seeming at once to be absorbed into an immeasurable depth and to be generated there as well.

Another month and she had almost achieved the eye-sun, a concatenation of shreds of cotton and aluminum wound inextricably together in a frayed circle concentric with, and glued to, the darkness surrounding it. Over this tangle of strips and coils and spirals she trickled gold house paint from two quart cans she had had mixed at the hardware store, the same day she'd gotten the tin snips for the aluminum scraps. The boy who had waited on her had kept his distance and spoken deliberately, as if he thought she was an alien child, or deranged, a madwoman who might go berserk suddenly if he made the wrong move.

She hadn't blamed him for this once she looked at herself in the bathroom mirror when she got home. Her dress, with its speckles of paint and little bits of scrap paper stuck randomly about, resembled one of her early collages. Above it, her face repeated the impression, more flamboyantly because of the smears of paint on her cheeks and forehead where she had drawn her hand across them, brushing her straggling hair aside, or trying somehow to wipe away the blind spots in her eyes. By now the spots had enlarged so much she had to aim her head at the corner of the bathroom, forcing herself to focus there, before she could see her face, poorly, in the mirror.

"Clown," she said aloud. "Nothing but a clown."

But her eyes burned with another name. She felt it stall in her chest before it could rise and form a growl in her throat. The precise expression evaded her, but when she gave in to the muscular pressure of years of habit and looked directly at her reflection, it seemed for an instant she had set the beige opacities into two wells of molten flame.

She went back to her art as if she'd seen nothing.

She spent a sleepless night on the floor beside the bed, while the gold paint she had dripped on the central tangle of aluminum and cloth dried. It formed a complex threaded overlay, some of which sagged like miniature power lines into the gaps between the thin coils of metal. When she had fitted the top of the can into its paint-clogged groove she had thought she was finished, but something nagged at her and pushed her away, alternately making her want to stare a hole through this hodge-podge in her skewed way, and to turn her back on it and never look at it again.

Laboriously she shoved the bed farther from both walls so she could walk around it more easily, looking at her creation from every degree of its horizon.

She mixed a cup of cobalt blue watercolor and with her smallest brush flipped specks of it on the eye-sun. She sprinkled a deeper metallic blue glitter on that, and then spent hours blowing it into different configurations until most of it disappeared in the maze. Lightheaded, she sat on the chair by the deserted table, leaning her cheek against one of the upper legs.

She stared into the corner beyond the bed. She thought of nothing. She longed to have her hands in mounds of cool lettuce. She saw herself serving drumsticks to hordes of picnicking children, their hands fluttering before her like finches. She saw Serena waltzing in her palace ballroom. Martin Luther King saluted her from the cockpit of his P-51. She blew him a kiss, told him she was sorry but she had to go down in the mine. The face of an anonymous lover flickered on and off like a neon sign, black light. She saw nothing.

When she finally closed her eyes she realized what was wrong, why she had drawn herself so near to completion but had driven herself with equal force away from her gift.

Of course.

So simple.

She had reversed the dark and light. The coal at the center of her vision and Christ's eye had become in her collage the surrounding, multilayered darkness. Her fire, instead of consuming, was about to be swallowed up.

Quick.

She got out of the chair, slumped externally, and borne so deeply into herself by the gravity of her realization that had there been one more step between her and the newly shifted bed she would have crumpled to the floor. As it was she fell into the collage, curling with her last energy around its center, feeling nothing, not even the pain in the part of her side that crushed some of the sharp-edged tines of the aluminum.

A few days later Serena Peoples would open the unlocked door of Mariah's apartment and find her sitting on the side of the bed, her head tilted toward her shoulder, staring at the bare window, sightless, one side of her mottled dress torn slightly and stained more deeply than the rest, the huge collage behind her bearing the rumpled imprint of her body, her shadow obscuring the cracked sunburst from which she seemed to have risen.

The Air Ghosts Breathe

HE DIDN'T like to be called Tidewater.

"Ain't my name," he'd say. But he'd say it rarely, as if he knew it was likely no one was listening to him. His friends called him Willy, or Parole, but the white people he dealt with in his work needed a shield against such a straightforward nominal approach to who Willy Parole might be, so they called him by a nickname one of them had invented too long ago to trace.

He thought, too, that people who said *Tidewater*—not just as a way to call him, but as a designation of place—seemed unconcerned about words themselves. It was partly a matter of imprecision: Atlantic City and Charleston and My-me Beach were Tidewater cities—he knew about them from some of the sailors who came into Sam Oakley's roadhouse—so saying you lived in Tidewater didn't exactly fix your position on the map. This part of the problem had gotten worse as the small towns he'd known as a child and young man—Phoebus, Hampton, Newport News—had, under the pressure of an expanding military population, burgeoned and begun to merge at their fringes into one huge mass. The old boundaries were disappearing too fast for him, and the insidious growth of his confusion about this—the shape of his home ground—intensified at the sound of *Tidewater*.

"I live in Tidewater," people would say. But Willy lived in Fox Hill. He didn't know in any way that mattered to him where "Tidewater" was.

As important as he considered this dislocation, he puzzled just as deeply over people seeming not to care about how words lived in what they named. At first he tried to joke about it.

"Anybody live in Tidewater must be pretty wet," he'd say. Or, "What white folks do with that mud when the tide's out?" He could hold his whiskey, but sometimes when the red-eye was bucking him like a sharp-spined stallion, he'd push the limits of his wit, too.

"Yeah," he'd say, sitting in Sam Oakley's roadhouse, "you know how slimy them flats get. Spread out like Satan's trots." He'd stretch his right arm and draw a semicircle over the table, smoothing the cigarette smoke languidly unfurling in the air. "Looks black, but got that slime green color in it. Pick it up with a pitchfork and you got long stringy globs of it." He might rise and go through the motions of digging, or pause and stare into the colorless fire in his jelly glass. "Greenblacks. Haw! Can't spend it. Can't eat it. Can't even bale it up and sell it. No, nor all the trash buried in it, neither."

He'd pause. He'd take a taste. Then his face would expand as if he'd remembered something. "They too *clean* to live in *Tidewater.*" He'd elongate the first syllable, skating on it. "Get down in *that* muck, they have to spend all their time scrubbing just to get ready to walk downtown."

But the joking only hinted at his perplexity. If *Tidewater* didn't refer to bodies of water the tide pulled in and out, then what *did* it do? You could swim in tide water, row a boat on it, drop your line in it, and take eels and swelltoads and spot from it. You could watch the sun rise and set on it, casting its bright track from your feet all the way to the horizon. It was everywhere ocean and sea and sound and bay met the land, not only at Old Point and Willoughby Spit, but on the coasts of all the Caribbean islands, and Africa, too. Had to be salt water, Willy knew that, though he had heard another word for salt and fresh mixing way upstream in the rivers.

Brackish. That was it. He wondered what brackish water tasted like.

But if you took a word away from what it named—if you said you *lived* in *Tidewater*—you threw everything off-kilter. Words became a quicksand which could swallow you up, or a game you played whose rules shifted every time you said something. The terror lurking in such speculation was enough to drive a man to church.

Willy Parole had been to church some when he was a boy, but not because his parents took him. His mother spent Sundays in bed, not alone, taking advantage of his father's weekend binges, which left him sprawled and oblivious in nests of "young thangs," as he called them, almost anywhere on the Peninsula from Williamsburg to Newport News. His ability to show up at the drydock company for work on Monday morning was as legendary as the exploits that rendered it implausible, and led to his nickname, Phoenix. ("My father's a bird," Willy would say, after he learned what *phoenix* referred to, and later, more sardonically, "a bird with a bird.")

Rumford "Phoenix" Parole died when Willy was sixteen, from lockjaw consequent on infection from an untreated cut on his forearm. He was thirty-five. It was a disappointing death, preempting possibility and fulfillment; no one would ever know how long he could have sustained his prodigious capacity for pleasure and recuperation, and his legend had no fitting cap, no ecstatic expiration at the moment of climax among a bevy of his doves.

In his late boyhood and early teens, then, Willy didn't go to church because of family pressure—there were no grandparents either, to step into the parental vacuum. He went because some of his friends were made to go, and he liked their company better than the effort it took to ignore his mother and her Sunday man who, in their sexual and alcoholic stupor, were themselves only vaguely aware of his presence.

Or absence.

Willy found out in ten minutes of his first church service that he couldn't sing. He listened to his voice, not yet stressed by puberty, wander about on the melody, as erratic and unpredictable as a swallow's flight. In fact, he wondered whose voice that was, rising and falling across the smooth career of everyone else's harmony. After two hymns he had to acknowledge it as his own, however, and from then on he sang in a throaty whisper, making a muted background drone that would have functioned as a bass line had his voice been deep enough.

His disappointment, though penetrating, was brief, like the pain from an open-handed slap across the face. Singing occupied two-thirds of the service at Amps' Run Pentecostal Revelation and Holiness Church, and when Willy realized he couldn't soar on the music, he settled his entire attention instead into the words. Since he was not a believer, preconception, like mist on a windowpane, blurred neither their mystery nor his curiosity. He saw, for instance, the water and the blood running from Christ's side, and understood they were supposed to be the "double cure" of sin; how that worked exactly he puzzled over. Water could cure thirst and cool fever, but neither thirst nor fever seemed sinful to him. Of course, thirst was a kind of longing for something needful you didn't have; he could see that as a way of speaking about a need for Jesus, but *that* wasn't a sin either. Was it? Jesus wouldn't condemn you because you thirsted for him, would he?

As murky as his thoughts turned the water, he got nowhere with the blood. The idea of drinking it, as palpable to his imagination as the words on the page of the battered hymn book were to his eyes, nauseated him. Being washed in it—he figured that Jesus' blood and "the blood of the lamb" in another hymn must somehow be the same—repulsed him almost as violently. His skin shrank from the prospect. All around him people—including some friends his own age—were leaning and spiring to the music, their mouths and throats rhapsodic with the obvious delight their incantations both brought them and carried away into the dust-speckled shafts of sunlight slanting through the windows above their heads. He felt left behind, grounded, denied some fundamental concordance that they had been born to, or with, making their transport here as easy and natural to them as eating cornbread and beans would be two hours hence.

The roust and jostle of play after the congregation streamed from the double doors of the whitewashed, plank building and puddled randomly in the field around it afforded Willy some compensation for his displacement inside. Everyone else seemed to leave the sermon and the Bible responses and the singing behind, jolting loose from all that in their chasing and taunting and conspiratorial planning for the afternoon. Yet even here—himself embroiled, calling a name, dodging a tag—Willy heard echoes of the service, as if the sounds focused inside the church gradually dispersed in the air, much as the people themselves spread their delta outward from the entrance, eventually scattering, disjoined and separate, into their private distances.

He had pursued these occasional diversions for five years or so, as a person unaware of living in a balloon might now and then press tentatively against it, feeling its flexible membrane give just enough to imply that, even if he couldn't escape from it, he could alter its configuration. Then, approaching fourteen, wiry and strong and possessing a stamina that provided him the only apparent link to his father, he went to work.

During the week he apprenticed himself to whoever would take him on, asking only for lunch in return. In the two-and-a-half years before Phoenix Parole dragged his forearm across the rusted edge of a winch shank at the number ten railway, Willy became as adept a carpenter, plumber, and roofer, for repair work and small construction projects, as most any of his white mentors who listed themselves in the Yellow Pages. On Saturdays and Sundays, from the beginning, he did odd jobs and yard work, going from house to house asking what might need doing that he could manage. Early in the morning he would flag down the bus to Hampton, because he had found the neighborhoods there dependable for work; the people were nice to him, too, some of them saving specific chores for him after a while, gradually creating a regular pattern both they and Willy settled into, developing a mutual dependence.

He never missed a day. He liked working better than going to church, though sometimes—raking leaves, or rearranging the haphazard contents of someone's basement—he'd catch himself humming the words to a hymn, the discrepancy between the tune he traced in his mind and the barely modulated drone coming from his throat making him laugh to himself.

Once he must have approximated the tune more closely than usual because the woman who was fussing about her yard while he thinned daffodil bulbs chimed in on a chorus of "Amazing Grace." Then she began to sing a verse. Her voice was clear and sweet, like springwater. Willy fell silent. She noticed this and softened her volume, fading at the end of the verse, not picking up the chorus again.

"I'm sorry," she said, standing above him, but off to the side, her shadow falling across the garden cart and the bags of fertilizer and peat moss crimped and leaning like ripples against its sides.

Willy hadn't been sure what she was apologizing for, but he had raised his eyes from the flower bed, across the hem of her dress—the color he imagined the daffodils would be—and, looking at her right elbow, told her it was all right.

He had loved her singing. It had a severe yet affectionate clarity, unprecedented in his hearing, radically different from the hearty voices at church, rolling over each other, taking off into various side harmonies and such embroideries of air that sometimes it seemed the music boiled like a stew. This white woman's sound, isolated in her garden, resembled a thread drawn cleanly through the eye of a needle. It wasn't emotionless; it seemed rather that the woman had once felt something which the hymn expressed for her, but she had moved through it and was singing from another side. Or perhaps it had moved through her and what Willy heard was a balanced longing and resignation, distilled to an essence her voice recalled.

She had sung a verse he'd never heard, about being here ten thousand years. He could figure the sun—*bright shining* were the words he heard sewn by the silvery filament her throat spun outward—lasting that long, or longer, though he had heard it was just another star, boiling gasses that would eventually burn itself up. A people living that long, though, staggered his mind, made it totter and sit down in its own shade, so to speak, and refuse to continue the thought.

Willy lived in the moment; he was present tense. He had no particular truck with his brief past which, when it presented itself to him, did so as an atmosphere—gray, undifferentiated—that he had managed so far to survive. Sparsely peopled, it hovered on the periphery of his imagination, not quite menacing, but capable, if he gave it too much attention, of coalescing into weather of serious implications—a whale of a storm that might swallow him up quick.

The future he avoided similarly—though in either case his will was less involved than his instinct—not because the projection of the details of his circumstances into the years ahead of him accumulated into a numbing routine more like a treadmill than a life. Such a prospect would not have daunted him. He considered the future, on the rare occasions he slanted his attention vaguely in its direction, as weather, too, but not the washed-out looming of the past. It was bright—*bright shining as the sun,* he could now say to himself—full of splendor a man could not look at directly because it would surely blind him, scald his eyeballs into blank, gray disks swimming in a milky paste, and char his brain to a flaky cinder.

Paradoxically, Willy imagined that spontaneity and unlimited potential filled this dazzle. An infinite, and infinitely subtle, weave of variation and surprise continually articulated itself, instant by instant, so infinitesimal at any given flick of time that no one could possibly discern it. This weaving was done with threads of light incessantly spun out of every person walking on the ground, from Fox Hill to Toano to Providence Forge to Richmond to everywhere Willy had never heard of. It wasn't the fact of this light, itself imperceptible, that was blinding; it was the sheer unpredictability of the patterns it accomplished. Nobody was ever *ready* to look ahead. You saved your life by living it.

By his sixteenth year Willy had developed a substantial network of people who looked for him regularly, or who called him about problems when they arose. He stationed himself by the telephone booth outside Sam Oakley's on week days, rain or shine, between 7 and 8 A.M., the period during which he told his customers to call him for emergencies, or special needs. No one came to the roadhouse in the morning, but occasionally he would hear Sam knocking around inside, getting his breakfast, or cleaning the place up. If the phone rang he'd schedule whatever came up around the commitments he'd already made. By the time he was twenty and had his own apartment and telephone, the roadhouse had become so widely known as "Willy's Office" that Sam had had a sign put up calling the place just that. Six feet high, it stretched the length of the ridgepole; after the red lettering on the right end Sam had a telephone receiver painted, standing vertical like an exclamation point. Only a few people remembered any more what the designation had referred to originally; Sam's clientele kept shifting, almost month by month after a while. When word got around about the blues music some of his friends used to play spontaneously simply as part of the genial spirit of being there, small squads of white men stationed at the nearby military bases began to wedge in. A cover charge followed soon after, as this infiltration increased and became predictable. Sam levied it on the whites only even though the sign on the door made it seem an even-handed policy. It enabled him to pay the musicians, and eventually to add a room to the building.

Willy's role as a regular drinker at his old "office" commenced two decades after all this, however, when Sam Oakley himself was gone—his name still alive, though, in Willy's mind, capable of conjuring Sam's image in the early morning fumes of rotgut and memory ghosts are rumored to breathe—and the heyday of the place was over. But at sixteen he didn't have time for more than an occasional beer in the evenings. His work didn't allow it; he was, in his own way, too successful to slow down.

Among the half-dozen families in Hampton to whom Willy began to commit the majority of his scheduled time, the Marshalls engaged him most often, offering him interesting and varied challenges, from which he learned more than all his other repeat situations put together.

The old woman who had hired him at first, when he was scrounging handyman labor, had given him mostly hauling and heavy yard work. He had bailed out her fish pond, set in a spot in the far back garden shaded by what he learned later were fig trees, and remortared its stones, in the process installing a drainage pipe and bung that would simplify cleaning the pond in the future. When he revealed similar initiative and imagination in other apparently routine jobs, she had given him increasingly more responsible assignments, instructing him less at the outset and leaving decisions as they arose in the course of projects pretty much to him.

He welcomed these developments, partly because he hadn't expected them, but he suspected the old lady gave him his head for reasons other than her recognition of his disparate skills. She was an aloof person, who emitted an aura of being somehow inherently eminent. She disguised badly her condescension to him—and, he thought after a while, probably to almost everyone—pointing frequently and then uncurling the rest of her fingers and waving them brusquely in the direction of the object as if to dismiss it, always a sign for Willy to get to work. His increasing independence, then, once she had set him a particular task, he felt was essentially an expression of her relief at not having to deal with him so directly.

He didn't like her. He didn't like white women in general—at least the middle-class ones he did business with—and she took some of their most vexing characteristics to extremes. She was vain about her clothes, for example, having a special outfit for everything. When he arrived for work in the morning she had on a dress of some subdued color, usually a dark shade of blue, but when she came to the yard a half hour later to check up on him she wore an older print that looked like it had been made of draperies like the ones in her living room. At eleven she left for the morning—to shop, to call on friends—decked out in bright green or orange, the skirt flaring perkily. She had shoes for every hour, it seemed to him, and an endless array of flower- and fruit-bedecked hats she wore as often in the house as out, even when she was alone.

She matched the changes of clothes with shifts in attitude. Businesslike and dismissive with Willy, she became a flurry of strut and priss when she navigated the flagstone walk to the car to go downtown. Willy had helped Delia Walker, her cook and maid, serve dinner on some party occasions, and he had watched her preside like royalty over her end of the long, oval table.

"All she needs," he'd say at the roadhouse, "is a scepter to wave. She holds her head like they's a crown already on it."

Centering the whole ritual of pretense was her way of pursing her lips slightly and daubing at the corner of her mouth with her napkin, poised negligently on the forefinger of her right hand, flicking her eyes to the left at the precise instant linen grazed flesh, as if the encounter were too delicate to witness. The first time Willy observed this he barely stifled his laughter, turning back to the sideboard and resettling the tray of finger bowls, pretending to rearrange them.

"You *know* she practices that in front of that big mirror upstairs. Whoeee." Everyone would watch in silence as he took an exaggerated sip of whiskey, holding his elbow out above the table, bringing his glass around in a slow arc, stretching his neck out like a crowing rooster to meet it. Then he extended the caricature to include Mrs. Marshall's gesture, setting his glass down, raising his eyebrows, dotting his lips with the loose cuff of his shirt sleeve. Invariably his performance brought the house down, his own laughter rich in the smoke-laced air.

Being black, and adept at hiding behind the poses he had quickly learned white people expected to see, and themselves projected outwardly to screen the world, helped him treat the old lady with the deference she believed necessary, not only for local but cosmic harmony as well. But he would have behaved courteously toward her anyhow, as it turned out, because of his growing affection for her husband.

Once Willy had organized the seasonal yard chores into a routine, Mr. Marshall had gradually taken over as the one who prescribed his other work. This meant Willy had to get to Hampton a little earlier on the days he went to the Marshalls' because the old man left for his insurance office at 7:30. He adjusted to the change with little complaint, however, when he realized it involved dimensions more important than the clock's.

The old man looked him in the eye when they talked. Willy knew without being told that if he needed help with something new to him he could ask for it, and not be treated like a subhuman idiot. Mr. Marshall's way of instruction was to demonstrate a procedure and then watch Willy repeat it, commenting, reminding, focusing, often asking Willy why he did this or that as he went along.

Much of this energy went into the engine in the old man's Nash, a sleek maroon-and-cream sedan Willy also Simonized once a month. Sometimes Willy would arrive and find Mr. Marshall under the hood, tinkering, as he liked to call it. Willy's natural curiosity led him to watch at first, and before long his employment at the big Victorian house on the spit had become partly a course in automotive repair. Words he had never heard before—*piston ring, intake valve, differential*—seemed after a while to inhere in the oil-slick or gunky parts that passed between him and this man who had taken him on as a student, or a partner—often he couldn't have said which. Sometimes Mr. Marshall became engrossed in the evolution of a particular repair, talking to the engine and himself and Willy in the same amiable tone—cajoling, considering alternatives, testing—as if they were all cogs in a larger enterprise whose smooth running depended in turn on their complex cooperation. Willy fit right in.

When it came time for Mr. Marshall to clean up and walk to his office, Willy could feel the falling away of his interest, a noticeable roughening of his smaller movements, as if the gestures in an animated cartoon had suddenly become less minutely drawn, a frame omitted now and then. The old man was as courteous and straightforward as always to Willy, but he was less *present.* Though the two of them never talked about this, Willy realized Mr. Marshall had to push himself through a barrier when he passed from the garage to his insurance business.

Once, some years after his father died, lying on his cot in the shack he'd rented out the road toward Seldon's dairy farm, he'd wondered what it would be like to share a real automobile shop with Mr. Marshall, be partners on paper as well as in spirit, do business in public. He'd held his hand up in the twilight, looking at nothing but its color. He hadn't smiled, or let himself feel any-thing. A plane had landed across the road at the testing grounds. He got up and stood in his open doorway, looking at the wind tunnels set on their struts; they resembled a carnival ride, and he imagined himself suspended in one of them, the wind machine propelling air past him so fast he disintegrated, became dust in the deafening swirl.

As the old man wiped the cleaner from his hands—pulling the rag along each outstretched finger with the same attention he worked on the engine—he outlined for Willy the day's work, asking his opinion on the size of a pipe or the angle of a brace, checking the progress of whatever task Willy might be in the midst of. Then he would walk the flagstones to the house, leaving Willy to gather the tools he needed. When the old man left for downtown Willy would usually be settled in to work out of sight of the gate to the gravel lane to Queen Street and downtown. But he had seen Mr. Marshall through the series of glass panes in the roll-up garage door often enough to know how smartly he dressed, regardless of the weather. He always carried an umbrella or a cane, flicking the tip with a casual precision against the gravel, and then up and in front about thirty degrees. He wore his three-piece suits with the same ease he moved in his coveralls. Willy figured he worked amiably with the people at his office, no matter how that situation differed from the one which he shared with Willy.

"Ever done any outdoor plumbing?" he asked Willy one day in early May, beginning the third year of his working at the Marshalls'.

"No, sir. Evvything's been inside so far."

The two of them stood outside the yard door to the Marshalls' garage, the entrance to the storage end of the L-shaped building. Willy looked over the clusters of various species of daffodils, the rows of peonies and hyacinths, and the camellia bushes that wound among the beds. He took pleasure in his part in the abundance and harmony of the rich blossoming before him.

Mr. Marshall pointed across the expanse of Spring colors and moved his arm from left to right, indicating the six-foot board fence that screened his property from the struggling, single-rail drydock next door. Its green planking ran the entire 250 feet from the house behind his garage to the breakwater at the bay end of his front lawn.

"I want to run a water line from the main to the boathouse. You know where the main comes in." He swung his arm to the basement bulkhead making its squat triangle against the side of the house. "What do you think about T-ing off it there, taking a 90-degree turn about a foot shy of the fence, and running the new pipe down the fence line to the dock?"

Willy walked to the bulkhead, which he noticed needed a new coat of paint itself, and let his gaze make the trip along the ground at the base of the fence.

"We'd have some roots to cut," he said, nodding at the bushes Mrs. Marshall had put in some years ago to break up the monotonous extension of the old boards.

"I'll bet you would've like to cut some of them when you rebuilt the fence last year," Mr. Marshall said. He had followed Willy across the yard and was standing beside him again.

"Wasn't so much the fixin' they bothered, as it was the painting," Willy said. "I reckon it's a good thing bushes are green."

They kept silent for a while, the early morning air softly rippling their shirts. At the end of the fence sunlight skittered on the water.

Beside it the weathered dock stretched its gray stripe from the cement breakwater to the Marshall's boathouse.

"You figurin' to clamp the pipe to the dock joists?" Willy asked.

"Good idea," Mr. Marshall said. "Then run it up through the boathouse floor. We can decide when we get out there exactly where the sinks ought to go."

It looked like a straightforward job, though setting up access to shut-off and drainage valves might be a little tricky, and there was no telling how ornery the root systems would be. Before they turned away to their separate undertakings, however, Willy mentioned the one difficulty they had both overlooked, probably because it was troublesome enough to make them consider scuttling the project.

"We going over the breakwater, or through it?" he asked.

The old man smiled. "You built it," he said. "What do you think?"

"Ain't no bit long enough to drill it," Willy said. "Even coming through both sides, still be a foot or so left in the middle." Willy considered the breakwater, remembering his long hours tearing out the old, wooden one, Mr. Marshall's grandson "helping" him, asking questions half the time, the other half seeming to brood on some deep mystery. He had struck Willy as a strange child, until he did the normal thing and threw up at the sight of the eels Willy began to haul out from behind the rotting planks.

Willy and the old man walked the length of the sloping yard, their shoulders dappled by the sunlight filtering through the leaves of the giant elms spreading their vase-shaped elegance above them. The surface of the top of the breakwater seemed otherworldly in its brightness, a two-foot-wide band of chalky sheen between the still green of the grass and the murky slap of the bay against its face.

They stared at this obstacle, then at the boathouse, and finally at the mouth of the small bay giving into Hampton Roads.

"What Mrs. Marshall goin' to think about messing with her bushes?" Willy asked, pressing the toe of his shoe into the crease where the grass met the breakwater.

"I'll talk to her before I leave. You go ahead and start digging at the bulkhead."

It turned out Willy compromised between going over or through the cement. He jackhammered a six-inch-deep, V-shaped groove into the top of the breakwater next to the dock, laid the bright copper pipe in it, and covered it over. After it cured, the patch, smooth and neatly troweled, matched almost perfectly the color of the original mix.

The ground work, though, gave him more trouble than he'd anticipated, taking nearly two weeks before he could begin laying and soldering the sections of the pipe, extending the whole job well beyond the time either he or Mr. Marshall expected it to take. Once he resigned himself to the inevitable, however, the manipulation of the spade and his other tools developed a pattern he settled into with a kind of pleasure. On the evening of the second day Mr. Marshall had proposed he quit digging and lay the pipe on the ground—"It's going to be exposed past the breakwater anyhow. We can keep it covered with mulch or something"—but Willy had convinced him it wasn't as wearing as it looked, and they adhered to their initial plan.

Willy loved the rhythm of labor that engaged his whole body, gave himself to it in the same way he abandoned himself to the drift and slide of sleep. Swinging the ax or mattock against the roots he exposed—some two or three inches in diameter, angling horizontally across the narrow ditch he opened—released his mind, letting it wander from immediate sensation to a series of random images that seemed connected by nothing but their own shapes, a kinship like his dreams built for him in the early mornings. Sometimes a word would float up from the unfolding mirage, a piece of a jigsaw puzzle detaching itself from the jumble and taking verbal shape in the air, or in his ear, for often he would hear rather than see the word, the visual part of his revery going blank, or settling into a beige or ice-blue flatness, like an empty screen.

The experience reminded him of the hymns he had heard and tried to sing in church, the rhythm of his body's motion coupled with the pattern of images which were a kind of music, all issuing in words, though he admitted none of it made the sense the hymns made. Yet he often found himself humming when he laid the ax aside, and whether he brought a word back with him or not, he felt filled with his revery, with his journey inward.

Time sang by for him. He'd come to his lunch break as if he'd risen into it from his cot. He would eat his cheese sandwiches and fruit and potato chips, washing it all down with water from the hose spigot he'd installed near the fish pond. Sitting with his back against the fence, which afforded some noon shade, he'd doze off for a few minutes, sometimes lulled by the railway engine cranking a boat up or down the reverberating chain, or the sound of the mallets wedging the devil into the hull. He'd look across the inlet beyond the house next to the Marshalls' and his eyelids would lower slowly, fuzzing the brightly painted water side of Hartog's crab works.

He accepted no other work during the six weeks or so he was involved with getting the pipe to the boathouse and the sinks installed. As he nosed the ditch down the last third of the yard toward the breakwater, he had slipped into the day's routine as completely as he had earlier welcomed his body's repetitive activity. The midday suspension became a beat in the rhythm of his labor, similar on a more extended scale to the pause at the top of his swing when the ax hung momently in the air and his muscles infinitesimally relaxed, before gathering again for the downward arc of the blade.

One Friday, feeling the warmth of the fence board against the back of his head and neck, he slipped into a picture of himself helping to load a freight car. It began in part as a memory of the time he'd taken the bus to Richmond, to the wholesale district in the James River bottoms near the canal, to help Mr. Marshall's son-in-law get out a rush shipment of appliances. But from the beginning, too, it was his usual daydreaming, as if a film reeled itself out across the inside of his eyelids, his mind playing games on a membrane he made accessible by closing them.

He straddled the edge of a freight car, one foot inside, the other on the loading dock. Through the gap between he could see the gravel mounded under the dark ties. He smelled creosote, sharp, invigorating. It was midnight, but a thin, coppery light pervaded the warehouse, washing the endless stretch of cartons stacked to its far walls, and the smaller version of that tableau slowly filling one end of the freight car.

Willy received a carton from the man on his left and passed it to the man inside the car, neither of whom he actually saw. He was, in fact, alone, though he knew a chain of men extended from the loading dock into the depths of the warehouse. He saw into the cartons, too—corrugated, impermeable—identifying washers, driers, small refrigerators and space heaters, yet when he hefted them they weighed no more than a bird's cage.

A swaying, thumping beat accompanied the passage of the cartons, as if they initiated it, the deep, percussive sound emerging both from their swinging movement from invisible man to invisible man, and from their separate interiors. Willy felt the beat in his feet, in his pelvis, in his throat. He was buoyed by it. He rode it. He absorbed it.

And was standing on a trapeze swing suspended in a large cage whose thin, glittering bars he could barely distinguish from the amber air. He held the ropes on either side, his arms raised, his head lifted. He hummed. He felt the humming rise from his groin, up through his chest and teeth, and pass outward into the wiry bars until they shimmered with it.

He was the hummer in the cage and he hugged the cage to himself, thrummed by it, carrying it into the freight car, which became a boat on the misted river, an amber twilight.

Invisible presences, helpers, hovered above him, the audience of his transport, the choir among whom he would eventually take his place, lifted into their music, breathing it, bringing into himself its warmth, its pulse, its settlement.

But the boat jarred against a rock, throwing him, still holding the cage of himself, into the flaky, gray water, which was a ground on which he sat, empty, empty-handed, looking at the strange gash on the inner length of his right forearm.

He dipped the tip of his left forefinger into the ripple of blood rising from the cut. He touched it to each of his eyelids, and to his lips. He brought his wounded arm, pure blood, around himself and around himself until it embraced him wholly, and whatever he saw or tasted was filmed with the blood of his lost, caged song, whatever it gave him.

The word he heard on the threshold of return was *welcome.* On the dreamside he said the word—*welcome*—to himself and to the pale blank shimmer he waved goodbye to. When he raised his lids to the wall of Hartog's far building and the nearer sights of breakwater and grass and the small ditch at his feet, he was murmuring to himself *home, home, home.*

Phoenix Parole's funeral and wake filled a day, and spread its amiable drunkenness well past midnight, though by then Willy had long since gotten a ride back into Hampton where he spent the weekend with a friend. Distributed lavishly on tables outside the church were roast pig and cornbread, casseroles of chicken and corn and mushrooms, messes of greens boiling on portable sterno burners, and pots of beans. People milled around and picked food off paper plates while a man—short, burly, ageless—Willy had never seen delivered a farewell to his father. He was not a preacher; he wore an open collar, blue shirt, and overalls, though his wing-tips were polished to a high gloss. He read from a yellow paper he pulled out of his hip pocket and unfolded. He turned sideways to the sun, but still squinted against its glare.

Willy didn't hear a word he said.

Some women spoke to him, placing a hand on his arm, whispering solemnly through their crimson lipstick words about his sorrow and bereavement. His mother sat with him for ten minutes in the church, stuffy and stale with the summer heat. She said nothing much, but he was aware she was trying to comfort him, or fulfill her sense of her place in such an occasion to offer him comfort. A tall, angular man with a scar running down his cheek came and stood in the doorway, and she patted Willy on the shoulder as she left.

He watched the coffin lowered on its straps into the ground, one of the pall bearers involuntarily grunting with his effort to keep it level and not release its weight too soon. The real church preacher read something from a black book with a thin purple sash hanging from it.

What struck Willy most, who had already said goodbye to his father when he was alive, was that no one sang anything. As the coffin went, by the easing of its bearers, down into the sandy hole, the only sound accompanying it was the rush of traffic from the new highway off to the west. Though it was only midafternoon when Phoenix's body was laid to its rest, the traffic was a continuous race of noise that had in it not the remotest hint of melody or rhythm, or of anything measured by lapse and accent. It roared on, undifferentiated.

The small thump of the coffin, slightly tilted, hitting bottom was barely audible, as if it were the background shushing and the sound of the vehicles in the distance the solid, dominant presence at this going out of life.

For Willy it was the sound of *Tidewater,* the anonymous grounding of his displacement. He wondered, if someone called him from a distant town and asked him where he was, what would it mean for him to say *here.*

Acknowledgments

I N D I F F E R E N T forms, sections of this manuscript first appeared in the following journals: part of the third section of the title story as "A Field of Lupines" in *Boulevard;* the fourth section of the title story as "The Way to Cobbs Creek" in *The North American Review;* "Mariah" in *TriQuarterly;* "Bright Wings" in *The Kenyon Review.* I'm grateful to the editors for their permission to reprint this material.

I am also grateful to Washington and Lee University for a sabbatical during which I composed the first drafts of these fictions.

About the Author

W. Patrick Hinely, Washington & Lee University

D A B N E Y   S T U A R T   is the author of more than a dozen books of fiction, poetry, and criticism, including *Long Gone* and *Second Sight: Poems for Paintings by Carroll Cloar* (University of Missouri Press). He teaches at Washington and Lee University in Lexington, Virginia.